A BUSINESS CAREER

A BUSINESS CAREER

Charles W. Chesnutt

EDITED BY MATTHEW WILSON AND MARJAN A. VAN SCHAIK
INTRODUCTION BY MATTHEW WILSON

UNIVERSITY PRESS OF MISSISSIPPI   JACKSON

www.upress.state.ms.us

The University Press of Mississippi is a member of the Association of
American University Presses.

Copyright © 2005 by University Press of Mississippi
All rights reserved
Manufactured in the United States of America

Print-on-Demand Edition

Library of Congress Cataloging-in-Publication Data

Chesnutt, Charles Waddell, 1858–1932.
A business career / Charles W. Chesnutt ; edited by Matthew Wilson and
Marjan A. van Schaik ; introduction by Matthew Wilson.— 1st ed.
p. cm.
ISBN 978-1-60473-257-3 (alk. paper)
1. Women—Employment—Fiction. 2. Children of the rich—Fiction. 3. Loss
(Psychology)—Fiction. 4. Stenographers—Fiction. I. Wilson, Matthew, 1949–
II. Van Schaik, Marjan A. III. Title.
PS1292.C6B87   2005
813'.4—dc22   2004027255

British Library Cataloging-in-Publication Data available

INTRODUCTION

The publication of Charles W. Chesnutt's novel, *A Business Career*, along with its companion volume, *Evelyn's Husband*, sees the completion, with one exception, of the publication of the novels that Chesnutt left in manuscript.[1] In these fictions, Chesnutt is writing in the genre of the white-life novel, in which African Americans write exclusively about white experience. When Chesnutt completed these novels, this was a relatively new genre. In the late 1890s, Chesnutt and Paul Laurence Dunbar began, concurrently, to write white-life novels, and while Dunbar's were published, Chesnutt's have remained in manuscript for over a hundred years. A review of Dunbar's first white-life novel, *The Uncalled* (1898),[2] is revealing, for it helps contextualize the position of an African American who attempted to write white-life fictions in this period. "*The Bookman* for December 1898 objected to the characters in *The Uncalled*. Claiming that Dunbar should 'write about Negroes,' the reviewer lamented that 'the charming tender sympathy of *Folks from Dixie* is missing' and asserted that Dunbar was 'an outsider' who viewed his action 'as a stage manager'" (Williams 174). At the turn of the century, neither critics nor publishers nor white audiences were willing to listen to the voice of an

African American who had stepped outside what they assumed to be his "proper" role—as a writer who represented his own folk's experience, narrowly construed as rural and Southern, and as a race spokesman. The expectations that African American writers were to be representative remained much the same for the better part of a hundred years, and while there is no general consensus among the few critics who have written about the genre of the white-life novel, almost all assume that African American writers must serve as race spokesmen, a position diametrically opposed to what Chesnutt himself believed. He wrote, as he said in 1928, accepting the Spingarn Medal from the NAACP, "not as a Negro writing about Negroes, but as a human being writing about other human beings" (*Essays and Speeches* 514). From that subject position, his conviction was that he could write not only about African American experience, but also (and exclusively) about white experience.

Chesnutt's universalist subject position and his hope that his work could be received outside the matrix of race has been contradicted by the reception of and lack of attention to white-life novels. David Roediger has recently written that the "serious 'white life novel' has left very little impact on American literary criticism. Even its most spectacular successes, such as James Baldwin's *Giovanni's Room* or Zora Neale Hurston's *Seraph on the Suwanee*, are little read. Less artistically successful works, such as Richard Wright's pulpy and revealing account of loss and violence in the white middle class in *Savage Holiday*, vanish with hardly a trace" (8).

The neglect of the genre of white-life fiction is due to the persistence of the color line in literature. In 1928, James Weldon Johnson claimed that "white America has a strong feeling that Negro artists should refrain from making use of white subject matter. I mean by that, subject matter which it feels belongs to the white world. In plain words, white America does not welcome seeing the Negro competing with the white man on what it considers the white man's own ground" (479). The neglect of the genre has to do not only with the competition Johnson identified, but with a sense of imaginative trespass, as if, in the view of white readers, African American writers have had no right to represent white-life exclusively because to grant that right would be to acknowledge the permeability of the color line. Chesnutt himself commented on the presence of that heavily demarcated line when he wrote that Howells "has remarked several times that there is no color line in literature. On that point I take issue with him. I am pretty fairly convinced that the color line runs everywhere so far as the United States is concerned, and I am even now wondering whether the reputation I have made would help or hinder a novel that I might publish along an entirely different line" (Chesnutt, *Letters* 171). Of course, the novels "along an entirely different line" are his white-life novels, and until this day, the answer is that such works, at the very best, do not help the reputation of an African American writer.

That is not to say, however, that Chesnutt's ambitions in the white-life novels are the same as in his race fictions. In the white-life novels, he is clearly trying to write fictions that he hoped would become popular successes with a white audience. William L. Andrews is the only critic of Chesnutt to have mentioned them at any length, and he is unsympathetic. "Each of these undistinguished narratives," he writes, "had sprung from a similar motive—to write especially for the popular market—and each was concocted only after novel-length color line stories had failed to make headway either in the publishers' offices or in the bookstores" (*Literary Career* 131). Clearly, as Andrews argues, Chesnutt was trying, in these novels, to gauge the taste of his potential white audience and "to tailor a long work of fiction to the tastes of genteel readers" (122). In these works, Andrews claims, Chesnutt failed "to find . . . that spark of conviction and serious purpose which appears" in his race fiction (122).

But as we have begun to realize in recent years, the use of popular forms—the adventure, the romance, and melodrama—does not preclude serious cultural work. A popular genre, Hans Robert Jauss has written, fulfills "the expectations prescribed by ruling standards of taste, in that it satisfies the desire for the reproduction of the familiarly beautiful; confirms familiar sentiments; sanctions wishful notions . . . or even raises moral problems, but only to 'solve' them in an edifying manner as predecided questions" (25). The difficulty that Chesnutt had as a writer of popular forms is that he was never quite able to give himself over fully to those forms; he always adapted them in unexpected ways. Although he gave his readers the edification of happy endings in his romances, those endings were always packaged, generically, in ways designed to unsettle the reader.

The period in which Chesnutt worked on *A Business Career* was the heyday of the romance, the late nineteenth century, a time when "the romance became almost synonymous with the novel in the public mind and was the most popular form of reading matter" (Hart 183). In fact, as Grant C. Knight observed, "Nothing stands out more clearly in our literary history than the remarkable vogue of light romantic fiction in 1894, 1895, and 1896 . . ." (88), the years just preceding *A Business Career*, which was rejected by Houghton Mifflin in 1898. Most early commentators on bestsellers, though, (and this is the period in which the bestseller list was first developed) have talked in terms of escapism and reflection, suggesting that the writers of popular literature tried to assess and then mirror back to the public its own cultural common sense. But in recent years, we have begun to see that popular fiction also performs the function of constructing cultural common sense, that the writers of romance and their audiences are actively rather than passively linked, that writers, like Chesnutt, hope to collaborate actively with their audiences by pushing the envelope of the genre. When Chesnutt's first attempt at a bestseller opens, Stella Merwin, the central character, has finished her junior year in college, and being a practical girl, she has also just completed a course in shorthand. Stella is, then, a representative New Woman of the 1890s, a member of that generation of college women which caused much cultural anxiety in America at the turn-of-the-century, anxieties as mundane as those about the effect of women's education and as hyperbolic as the debate about "race suicide" (college women were assumed to be less fecund than their uneducated sisters). The New Woman has been defined as "a liminal figure between the Victorian woman and the flapper," who was "[s]ingle, white, affluent, politically and socially progressive, highly educated, and athletic" (Patterson 73). She was a "'pioneer [of] new roles able to 'insist upon a rightful place within the genteel world'" (Smith-Rosenberg qtd. in Patterson 73). Although Stella is not affluent, the novel records her return to her "rightful place" in the upper middle class, and she also demonstrates how she is a pioneer of new roles by going to work as a stenographer.

Chesnutt combines the romance of the New Woman with another genre, that of the working girl novel which was popular from 1880–1920. According to Christine Bold the genre usually centered on "a poor factory operative, shopgirl, or mill worker who manages to resist the unwelcome advances of the wealthy, upper-class villain, yet is often forced—unwittingly—into an illegal marriage with him, and finally ends the novel marrying an upper-class hero who admires her for her personal virtues that transcend her humble background" (297–98). Although there is only a suggestion in the novel of a leering villain (who Stella resolutely evades), she is recognized by her boss (and subsequent husband) "for her personal virtues," which combine the experience of working in an office with the college-educated wisdom of a New Woman.

Somewhat eccentric in its adaptation of the genre of romance, *A Business Career* fuses a New Woman fiction with the shopgirl novel. Dunbar's *Love of Landry* is, I would argue, much more representative of the romance in this period. That novel, set in Colorado, consists of a typical love triangle: a rich young woman, after refusing her British suitor, goes West for reasons of health and falls in love with a mysterious Westerner, Landry, who saves her life and who turns out to be a refugee from an old Eastern family. The British suitor follows her to Colorado where he bonds with Landry, and after a minimum of implausible impediments, Landry and the Eastern young woman announce their intention to get married.

A Business Career, on the other hand, involves the romance of an older man and younger woman (as do all of his white-life novels). Their marriage, however, is clearly marked in social terms, and Chesnutt is writing what has been called social melodrama, a genre "which synthesizes the archetype of melodrama with a carefully and elaborately developed social setting in such a way as to combine the emotional satisfactions of melodrama with the interest inherent in detailed, intimate, and realistic analysis of major social or historical phenomena" (Cawelti 261). Although Chesnutt sets the novel in "a great city of the Middle West" (1), a town he names Groveland, the events are temporally marked by reference to Sarah Bernhardt's 1891–1893 tour of the United States,[3] and by a number of other cultural references: to Sardou's *La Tosca*, which Stella Merwin sees in a performance by Bernhardt, and by references to Wagner, Padereski, and Shopenhauer among others. In the novel, then, Chesnutt grounds his melodrama in a realistic historical situation and gives his readers the dual pleasure of solving its problems in "an edifying manner" (Jauss 25) while giving them the satisfactions of realism.

Chesnutt wrote *A Business Career* in the years when he was struggling with his first race fiction, the novel that would become *The House Behind the Cedars* (1900) and when he was writing short fiction. He sent the manuscript to Houghton Mifflin along with a proposal for a book of short stories. Writing for the publisher, Walter Hines Page rejected both the novel and the proposed volume of short stories. "The novel," Page wrote, "we have regretfully come to the conclusion, would be a doubtful venture on our list. It does not follow, of course, that it would not succeed on some other list, for it might very well do so." He then goes on to talk about how "over-crowded" the novel market is, and he concludes that a "novel in these days must have some much more striking characteristic of plot or style to make its publication a good venture than was required a dozen years ago or less" (Helen Chesnutt 191). Two paragraphs later, Page returns to the idea of the novel's commercial viability: "the first of these propositions—that "A Business Career" may be a success—is not at all denied by Messrs. Houghton, Mifflin and Company's conservative attitude towards it. You will doubtless be able to find a publisher, and my advice to you is decidedly to keep trying till you do find one" (Helen Chesnutt 92). After this encouragement, though, Page suggested that Chesnutt put together a volume of conjure stories, which Chesnutt subsequently did. This pattern was to reproduce itself with each of Chesnutt's white-life novels: white editors always rejected his white-life fictions, preferring, instead, to have an African American write race fictions exclusively.[4]

Although this novel is being published a hundred years after Chesnutt wrote it, the larger question remains whether he was doing any more than cynically wearing the mask of whiteness as he tried to write a novel that he hoped would become a popular success. Is he, in the words of Addison Gayle, donning "the mask of white men, thus lending his own weight to the negative images which he despised, validating the arguments of those who championed the superiority of white images over those of blacks" (145)? The novel almost entirely ignores the presence of African Americans (there is one reference to a popular negro song, and Truscott's valet is a very dark African American), but I believe that Chesnutt saw his white novels, in part, as a way of escaping the burden of being representative, as a way of writing as if he were unraced. If he wrote his race fictions ". . . not primarily as a Negro writing about Negroes, but as a human being writing about other human beings" (*Essays* 514), then he is doing much the same thing in the white-life novels. As he did in his polemical writing, Chesnutt assumed that he possessed the same rights as white folks. Just as white writers had the right to represent black life, he assumed in his white-life novels that he had the right to represent white life. More importantly, though, Chesnutt believed that he did not necessarily have to be critical of white life, that he could represent white life in a popular genre without having to assume the burden of racial critique.

The publication of *A Business Career* rounds out our picture of Chesnutt's ambitions as a writer early in his career when he had published only sketches and short stories. In the years before the publication of *A House Behind the Cedars* (1900), Chesnutt was working simultaneously on two tracks: trying to write race fiction and white-life fiction. What unites those ambitions, however, is his preoccupation with female protagonists. In *A House Behind the Cedars*, Chesnutt is using the main female character to explore the state of racial liminality, of being caught between the black and white worlds, at ease in neither. In *A Business Career*, however, he was exploring a general state of dispossession; he placed Stella Merwin in a familiar setting and used her as a way to work through what must have been his own ambivalent feelings about his choices in life, about being dispossessed of rights and opportunities that he thought should have been his.

The publication of *A Business Career*, moreover, lets us see Chesnutt learning his craft as a novelist. Employing "social melodrama," Chesnutt learned how to saturate a novel with realistic markers while trying to imitate a popular genre. But even at this early point in his career, we see that Chesnutt felt a need to complicate that genre by overlaying it with cultural concerns about the New Woman, a sign that he will become increasingly unwilling to meet his readers' expectations. Most important, though, the publication of *A Business Career* allows us to gauge Chesnutt's subject position as a writer: from the beginning of his activities as a novelist, he assumed that he had the right, as an African American, not only to write for a white audience, but to write *about* white experience. By writing *A Business Career*, Chesnutt was claiming his rights as an *American* writer. By crossing the color line and writing white-life fiction, Chesnutt was hoping that he was wrong, that the color line did not run "everywhere as far as the United States is concerned" (*Letters* 171). Perhaps, the publication of this novel, over a hundred years after it was written, is evidence that the literary color line is in the process of slowly dissolving.

The publication of this novel of Charles W. Chesnutt would not have been possible without the support I received from the Pennsylvania State University. I received two grants from the Capital College Research Council and one from the Institute for Arts and Humanistic Studies of Pennsylvania State University. These grants allowed me to pay for the copying of Chesnutt's manuscript novels and to travel to Fisk University Library several times to work with Chesnutt's original manuscripts. I would like to thank the special collections librarians at Fisk for their help with my numerous requests. I would also like to thank John Slade for this kind permission to publish this manuscript novel of Chesnutt.

Note on the Text

The copy text for this edition is a typescript with handwritten revisions by Chesnutt in the Charles W. Chesnutt Collection, Special Collections, Fisk University Library, Nashville, Tennessee. The manuscript can be found in Box 7, folders 11–15. The manuscript is missing chapter XVI (pages 132–38), and it is also missing pages 185–86, but these omissions do not impede a reader's understanding of the plot.

The manuscript is heavily reworked: it underwent a major revision in pen and a later one in pencil. The manuscript alternates between pages that are heavily revised and pages that have hardly a mark on them. The pages with hardly a mark on them are a slightly different shade of white, and my conclusion is that Chesnutt had these pages retyped. The manuscript was clearly abandoned by Chesnutt before it reached its final form, and the heavy revisions in pen precede those in pencil, some of which were suggestions or queries to himself on which Chesnutt had not made final decisions. While I have corrected many errors in the typescript, I have retained some of Chesnutt's usages: his use of contractions is clearly inconsistent, and I have retained those inconsistencies. I have also retained Chesnutt's nonstandard, but correct spellings: e.g. "skilfull," "gravelled," "dishevelled."

Matthew Wilson

Notes

1. One more novel, *The Rainbow Chasers*, remains in manuscript. Chesnutt abandoned this novel before he fully worked out a revision of the plot, and were it to be published, it would need to be in a critical edition, where readers would be able to compare the two versions of the plot. A play, *Mrs. Darcy's Daughter*, also remains in manuscript.

2. Chesnutt owned a copy of Dunbar's *Uncalled* (McElrath, Chesnutt's Library 108).

3. Chesnutt lived in Cleveland where Bernhardt played in March 1892. Sardou's *La Tosca* was in her repertoire.

4. For example, Chesnutt's *The Rainbow Chasers* had been accepted for publication by Houghton Mifflin. Chesnutt also submitted *A House Behind the Cedars* in its place, and Chesnutt never returned to the revision of the white-life novel.

Works Cited

Andrews, William L. *The Literary Career of Charles W. Chesnutt.* Baton Rouge: Louisiana State UP, 1980.

Bold, Christine. "Popular Forms I." *The Columbia History of the American Novel.* Ed. Emory Elliot. New York: Columbia UP, 1991. 285–305.

Chesnutt, Charles W. *Charles W. Chesnutt: Essays and Speeches.* Eds. Joseph R. McElrath, Robert C. Leitz, III, and Jesse S. Crisler. Stanford: Stanford UP, 1999.

———. *To Be an Author: Letters of Charles W. Chesnutt, 1898–1905.* Eds. Joseph R. McElrath, Jr. and Robert C. Leitz III. Princeton: Princeton UP, 1997.

Chesnutt, Helen M. *Charles W. Chesnutt: Pioneer of the Color Line.* Chapel Hill: U of North Carolina P, 1952.

Gayle, Addison. "Literature as Catharsis: The Novels of Paul Laurence Dunbar." *A Singer in the Dawn: Reinterpretations of Paul Laurence Dunbar.* Ed. Jay Martin. New York: Dodd, Mead, 1975: 139–51.

Hart, James D. *The Popular Book: A History of America's Literary Taste.* New York: Oxford UP, 1950.

Jauss, Hans Robert. *Toward an Aesthetic of Reception.* Trans. Timothy Bahti. Minneapolis: U of Minnesota P, 1982.

Johnson, James Weldon. "The Dilemma of the Negro Author." *American Mercury* 15 (1928): 477–81.

Knight, Grant C. *The Critical Period in American Literature.* Chapel Hill: U of North Carolina P, 1951.

McElrath Jr., Joseph R. "Charles W. Chesnutt's Library." *Analytical and Enumerative Bibliography* 8 (1994): 102–19.

Patterson, Martha. " 'Survival of the Best Fitted': Selling the American New Woman as Gibson Girl, 1895–1910." *American Transcendental Quarterly* 9 (1995): 73–87.

Roediger, David. Introduction. *Black on White: Black Writers on What It Means to Be White.* Ed. David Roediger. New York: Schocken, 1998: 3–26.

Williams, Kenny J. "The Masking of the Novelist." *A Singer in the Dawn: Reinterpretations of Paul Laurence Dunbar.* Ed. Jay Martin. New York: Dodd, Mead, 1975: 152–207.

A BUSINESS CAREER

I.

In a large, handsomely appointed room on one of the upper floors of a tall office building in a great city of the Middle West, a gentleman sat at an open roll-top desk, somewhat impatiently opening letters with a carved ivory paper-knife,— a rather stern looking man, with a brown Van Dyke beard not too closely trimmed, which only partially hid an ugly scar on the left side of the lower lip. This scar gave, until one became accustomed to it, a somewhat sinister cast to an expression forbidding enough without it. The gentleman was of dark complexion, with coarse dark hair growing slightly grey about the edges, square shoulders and large hands. As he opened the letters, some he tossed carelessly into a gaping waste-basket, others he threw into an open drawer, and still others he laid in a pile on the table before him. One, a daintily scented note on tinted paper, in a feminine hand, he thrust into the breast-pocket of his coat. When he had thus gone through the letters he touched a button in the desk, and a moment later an office boy quietly entered the room and stood in an attitude of attention.

"Johnnie," said the gentleman, "has Mr. Peters been in this morning?"

"No, sir."

"Tell Mr. Ross to come here."

The gentleman's tone was as peremptory as his appearance would indicate. The office boy went out as quietly as he had entered, and a moment later a well-set man of medium height, apparently about forty years of age, with a mustache, a smooth-shaven chin, and a bald spot plainly visible on the top of his head, glided into the room with cat-like tread, and stood respectfully at the end of the desk.

"Mr. Ross, I understand that Peters hasn't shown up this morning."

"No, sir."

"He was late again yesterday morning?"

"Yes, sir."

"Has he sent any message?"

"No, sir, not this time."

"What is the matter with Peters?"

"Same old story, sir, I suppose. Saturday was pay-day, and he hasn't got over it yet, I guess."

"You have his address?"

"Yes, sir."

"Make out a check for three days' pay and mail it to him, with a notice that his services will no longer be required."

When the chief clerk had withdrawn, Mr. Truscott took up one letter from the pile before him and after studying it for a moment drew a sheet of paper in front of him, and taking up a pen began to write an answer. He had written only a line when he laid down the pen and again touched the button.

The office boy appeared as promptly as though the button had released a spring, which in turn had shot him into the room.

"Johnnie, get me some fresh ink."

"Yes, sir."

Johnnie had filled the inkstand that very morning, about half an hour before. But Johnnie was a shrewd boy and understood his business, and was familiar with his master's moods. He took away the inkstand, went into the next room, balanced the inkstand on the tips of his fingers, indulged in a *pas seul* that seemed to put the ink in imminent danger of spilling, and then walked gravely back into the other office with it.

Again Mr. Truscott took up the pen and began to write, and a moment later laid it down and touched the button.

"Johnnie," he said, "bring me a new pen."

A third time Mr. Truscott essayed to write, but the new pen, because of its smoothness, did not retain the ink, and before he had finished a line a large black drop slipped down to the point and settled upon the paper. Mr. Truscott impatiently doubled up the sheet, threw it into the waste-basket, and again touched the button, which the office boy sprang to answer.

"Call Mr. Ross," Mr. Truscott commanded. "Mr. Ross," he said to the chief clerk when that functionary had insinuated himself into the office, "I wish you would telephone up town to some shorthand office or typewriting bureau, and ask them to send me a stenographer for a day or two. Then advertise for an experienced male stenographer who does not drink. I've no time to waste with beginners or drunkards."

Then Mr. Truscott took up the morning paper and in a few minutes was deep in the financial news, while he awaited the arrival of the stenographer.

II.

For half an hour before Mr. Truscott had begun his morning's work, two women had been seated in an office a few blocks away from Mr. Truscott's. One of them was apparently anywhere from thirty-five to forty-five years of age, a short, stout woman, with strongly marked features of the German type. She wore gold-bowed glasses, a cloth suit with a short skirt, and radiated around her an atmosphere of bustling energy. The other was a slender girl, whose most salient features at first glance were an oval and somewhat pallid face, very large deep-blue eyes with long lashes, and more than usually abundant light-brown hair. One would say, from looking at her, that she was eighteen years old, or twenty-two, as one might be most impressed by the curve of her neck or the gravity of her expression; she was either younger than she looked, or looked younger than she was, depending upon the point of view. The two women were engaged in conversation, in which the elder took the lion's share. The younger woman was dressed with a quiet elegance which upon analysis would have seemed to be rather due to good taste than to expensive stuffs.

"And now, Stella," said the elder woman, "what are you going to do with your shorthand, since you've taken the trouble to learn it?"

"Oh, Mrs. Paxton," replied the young woman, "I shall find a use for it. I can take notes of lectures that I attend, I can keep my diary in it, I can correspond with you and I shall doubtless find it useful in the school-room. Besides, they talk of introducing shorthand into the public schools at Cloverdale, and in that event I shall stand first chance to become the teacher."

"I'm afraid of you, Stella. You're too good-looking to make a successful business woman. As soon as you've qualified yourself for independence, you'll throw yourself on the mercy of some man, who will crush all your higher aspirations and degrade you to the level of a mere housekeeper."

"There's no danger in my case, Mrs. Paxton. No man has ever tried to lead me aside from the path of independence. I shall probably have to earn my living, for mamma's income is small, and I could not dream of remaining a charge on her indefinitely. But I'm in no hurry; it will be a year yet before I'm out of college, and there will then be plenty of time for me to decide upon my future."

"You have talent enough and character enough, Stella Merwin, to take high rank in the sisterhood of progress. I feel that if I can just get you over the danger period, when a girl will marry any man who asks her, I can make you a noble exponent of the true doctrine that woman is man's equal, and can compete with him successfully in any sphere of intellectual or economic activity."

While Mrs. Paxton was speaking, the telephone bell rang and she went to answer it. Some one evidently addressed a question to her from the other end.

"Hello! Yes, I can send you our Miss Smith. Do you want her right away? Very well; I'll start her down in a few minutes."

"My assistant Miss Smith has gone down to take a letter for a gentleman in the block, and I am expecting her in every minute," she said to Stella, as she hung up the receiver. "Oh, dear me, there goes the bell again," she said before she had more than resumed her seat. "Hello! Is that you Miss Smith? Well, that's embarrassing. I was just going to send you out to another place for the day. But of course Mr. Bushnell has the first claim, since you are there already. All right, you stay."

"The gentleman she is working for will keep her busy for several hours, and I hardly know what to do about the other place. Oh! I have an idea! There's the chance of your life, Stella! I can send you down there, and it will give you some actual experience in short-hand work."

"Oh dear! Mrs. Paxton, I am afraid it wouldn't do. I'm only an amateur; I couldn't meet the requirements."

"I believe you could do anything, Stella Merwin, that you set your mind to. But there is nothing like being on the safe side. Just pull up that pad in front of you and take that pen and write from my dictation:

"The Truscott Refining Company,
    "City.
"Gentlemen:—This will be handed to you by Miss Merwin, who I trust will be able to do your work satisfactorily.
                                    "Yours truly,

"Now, sit down at this typewriter and run that out in your best style."

"That's very well done indeed," she said, when the result was handed her a moment later. "Education and all-round training always tell. Many a half-educated stenographer would not have written that short letter as neatly after three months of actual work. You have only made one mistake; you have written your name Smith instead of Merwin.

"Have I?" said Stella innocently. "Then let's leave it so. I'll be Miss Smith for today. Actors have stage names, authors have pen names. Let Miss Smith be my business name for today; I'll try not to disgrace it."

"Just as you please, my dear. Your face and figure will add distinction to the name. It is n't business-like, Stella—it's romantic, and romance is the death of business. But have it your own way."

Mrs. Paxton enclosed the letter and addressed it. She then gave Stella some brief directions about the details of office work, accompanied her to the elevator, and dismissed her with an encouraging word.

III.

While Stella Merwin is making her way through the busy streets to her destination it may be well to say a few words as to who she was and how she happened to be in the city and in Mrs. Paxton's office at this time.

Her father, Henry Merwin, had been, some years before, a successful and wealthy oil refiner of Groveland. Stella had been born in the city, and the first few years of her life had been spent amid surroundings of refined luxury. Her home had been on the beautiful Oakwood Avenue. Her father had kept fine horses and numerous servants, her mother had been popular in society; and Stella could distinctly remember how, when she was a child of six, the house had been aglow with lights and filled with gay company. She could remember, too, the fashionable private school not far from her own home, where she had learned her letters and to read words of one syllable. But while apparently at the height of his prosperity, Mr. Merwin had met with business reverses, or become entangled in financial difficulties, the nature of which had never been made quite clear to Stella, although her mother had often spoken of them. Indeed her mother's chief topic of conversation, outside of the routine affairs of daily life, had been, for fifteen years, her former social glory and the things that led to its eclipse. If Mrs. Merwin could have felt that her past was irrevocable, that her present reduced station in life was a finality, at least so far as any upward impulsion from the past was concerned, she might have been measurably contented, on the modest income which had been saved from the wreck. But the circumstances attendant upon her husband's failure had been such that she believed herself cheated of her rights, and had ever since cherished the hope of their restoration. Thus a sense of injustice, adding poignancy to griefs, and keeping alive regrets that time would otherwise have softened or dispelled, had warped and soured a naturally sunny disposition.

The main cause of Henry Merwin's downfall, and of his death shortly following it, was believed by Mrs. Merwin—and she had brought up her children to the same belief—to have been the conduct of a certain dishonest managing clerk, who had so ingratiated himself into Mr. Merwin's confidence as to gain complete knowledge of all his affairs and acquire such an ascendancy over his mind as to put the master entirely in the power of his subordinate. This clerk was ambitious and unscrupulous, and taking advantage of a financial flurry that laid his employer open to attack, had betrayed his interests, and by the basest treachery had ruined the man to whom he owed everything. For Henry Merwin had taken this boy into his office, the son of a poor widow, and had promoted him from office boy to clerk, from clerk to bookkeeper, from book-keeper to general manager. When the crisis came, and the business had to be sold to pay a judgment on a cognovit note, and the plant and good will were thrown on a congested market at a time when business confidence was shaken, few bidders had been forthcoming. The full measure of the clerk's iniquity was not at first apparent, and the betrayed master, even at this juncture, leaned upon and trusted this man. Mr. Merwin's business troubles brought on an acute nervous attack, and during the time he was confined at home as a result of it, his tangled affairs were left entirely in the hands of his manager, who spent much of his time by the sick man's bedside, in long confidential interviews, to which even his wife was not a party, and after which Mr. Merwin would for a while be soothed or elated, only to relapse again into still deeper despondency.

"I've made a mess of it, Alice," he once said. "If anything should happen to me, Wendell can tell you all. You will not be left destitute. He has papers that will make everything clear; he will give them to you. Forgive me, dear."

His wife had not loved him for his wealth, and assured him she had nothing to forgive; that misfortune might come to any one, and she would soothe his sorrows as she had shared his prosperity.

His forebodings had not been ill-founded. Before his affairs could be straightened out or closed up, he died, of heart disease, the attendant physician said. His wife had not known that his heart was weak, but the manager stated that he had been aware of it for several years, but that Mr. Merwin had carefully concealed it from his wife, in order to spare her feelings.

Mr. Merwin's manager took charge of the funeral arrangements, and relieved the widow of every care except her grief. After all was over, he seemed for a time almost her sole friend in her loneliness; for after her husband's failure her friends had not seemed so numerous as in more prosperous times. Perhaps it was because even in the brief time between the failure and Mr. Merwin's death, the family had been obliged to move to a less pretentious street than Oakwood Avenue, in a neighborhood with which the liveried coachmen of her wealthy acquaintances were not familiar enough to find her. Not only had few of her friends called, but some had given her scant recognition on casually meeting her, and one or two the cut direct. She did not hear, until some time later, that there were rumors of discreditable circumstances connected with her husband's failure, which might have influenced the conduct of her friends. For the few weeks following Mr. Merwin's death, when his young manager had listened to her complaints and excused, or palliated, or explained the conduct of her whilom friends, she had thought him the best man in the world.

Then had come the gradual awakening. In due time she began to think of the future, and at about the same time some ugly rumors reached her ears. She asked her kind friend for the papers of which her husband had spoken. He replied there were none; that he had no private papers of her husband, that were of any value whatever, and that none had been entrusted to his care for delivery to her.

"But," she said, surprised, "I do not understand at all. My husband told me, almost upon his death-bed, that you had papers that would clear up everything and save me and my children from want, and that you would deliver them to me with a full explanation."

"I'm sorry," he replied, gravely, "that he left you under any such impression. It is most distressing and most unfortunate. There will be a little left, but nothing that you do not know of already. Mr. Fitch, the executor of Mr. Merwin's will, is fully informed as to all the assets of the estate. He will bear me out in what I say."

Mrs. Merwin was not satisfied. She talked matters over with Mr. Fitch, her husband's attorney and executor, an old friend of the family, with no better results. Mr. Fitch thought there was no reason to doubt the integrity her husband's manager. There were several things that, to her mind, seemed to require explanation. Her husband had spoken to her, long before his failure, of certain stocks and bonds he had purchased and certain large gains he expected to make in some important enterprise not yet ready to be made public.

"We shall be rich, Alice," he had said with enthusiasm, "we shall be rich beyond the dreams of avarice. These paltry thousands for which I toil are a mere nothing compared to the fortune in sight for us. The little part I have taken in local business is but a trifling thing compared with the great rôle I am destined to play in the financial world."

It was undoubtedly to papers in connection with this matter that her husband had referred during his last illness. She could not understand how one so entirely in her husband's confidence as his manager had seemed to be, could possibly be ignorant of an affair of such consequence. Putting this and that together—things she had seen, others she had heard, in the course of the years that her husband and this man had been together, half-confidences that she had surprised—she began to doubt her husband's friend. Surely he must have known these things, and must now have some reason for concealing his knowledge. When, a few weeks after Mr. Merwin's death, his assets were thrown up on a disorganized market, and the former clerk bid in the plant for a song, and resumed the business on its former lines, she perceived at last the truth—that this was what her husband's manager, friend and confidant had all along aimed at,—to involve, to ruin her husband, that he himself might gather up the wreckage and gain control of the business on his own account.

She charged him with this perfidy, and the manner of his denial confirmed her belief. She had always been held a good judge of character. When she plied him with specific questions about the matter her husband had only hinted at, his visible embarrassment, his halting speech, showed, as clearly as if printed in a book, that he was concealing something. At Mr. Fitch's suggestion she consulted another lawyer, of her own selection. Her new adviser told her, after investigation, for which Mr. Fitch gave him every facility, that there was nothing tangible on which to act, and that, if her husband's late manager and successor had defrauded him or his estate, it had been so skilfully done and so carefully covered up that only time or accident would ever reveal the manner of it.

She wrote a long letter to this man, in which she implored him, in the name of the God of widows and orphans, to do justice to herself and her children. He replied in an ambiguous strain, denying that he had done them any wrong but offering to see that she and her children were provided for. She had refused his offer with scorn, spurning as a favor what she claimed as a right.

"I do not believe," she had written him, "that you will long enjoy your ill-gotten gains. God surely will not permit injustice to triumph forever. I shall yet live to see my husband's good name vindicated and my children restored to their own."

When the estate was finally settled, there remained enough, when skilfully invested and looked after by her late husband's executor, Mr. Fitch, to produce a small annual income, sufficient to maintain the family in very modest comfort in a small town not many miles removed from their former home. As time went on, Mrs. Merwin had turned her really fine mind to literary work, in a small way, in connection with a woman's journal, and had thereby added enough to her income to give her daughter Stella advantages of training and study otherwise beyond her means. Stella, bright and clever from infancy, had turned out to be all, or nearly all, that her mother could have wished. She had taken to books with avidity, and had learned music almost by intuition, had acquired languages with ease, and, in addition to all this, had found time to learn shorthand, and had learned also to manipulate with some degree of speed the little white-keyed machines that have made penmanship almost a lost art. In connection with these latter studies she had made the acquaintance of Mrs. Paxton, a wide-awake business woman, who conducted a short-hand school in Groveland, and in connection therewith a bureau for supplying office help. Stella had liked the bustling little woman, who had attained a fair measure of success under somewhat adverse conditions, and quite a friendship had sprung up between the two. It was during a trip to Groveland to visit her friend that the conversation with Mrs. Paxton already related had taken place.

This was Stella Merwin's personal history, as she remembered it, and her family history as she had learned it in far more voluminous detail, from time to time, from her mother's lips.

"Wendell Truscott," her mother had said to her only a few weeks before, with an earnestness of conviction intensified by fifteen years of brooding over her wrongs, "is a hypocrite and a villain. Your father, the kindest, and best, and noblest, and most confiding of men, trusted him implicitly. Wendell Truscott robbed his benefactor and ruined him, yes, murdered him, for he died of a broken heart! Not content with his work, he robbed the widow and the fatherless. Surely God will not let him go unpunished! Some time, in some way, perhaps from his own lips, perhaps by our efforts, perhaps by accident, the truth will become known, and he will be exposed to the scorn of all honest men; your father's memory will be cleared from all aspersions, and we shall have what is our own."

As Stella walked down the crowded street her eyes sought from time to time the address of the note she held in her hand—"The Truscott Refining Company."

Her father had been an oil refiner, and this must be the concern that had succeeded to his business. For "Wendell Truscott" had been the name of the dishonest manager who, since his assumption of the business, under a corporation of which he had speedily acquired control, had accumulated a great fortune and assumed a commanding position in the commercial world. While Mrs. Paxton was dictating the letter of introduction, Stella had doubted whether she should go or not, whether her mother would approve of such a step. But it was a very natural impulse for her to wish to meet their enemy face to face, and yet on his part unawares, under the incognito thus so conveniently provided. In spite of a very practical disposition, Stella could not help sharing in some degree her mother's belief in the ultimate triumph of justice. And it occurred to her that perhaps now this opportunity, which had seemingly arisen by the merest accident, might open up a way by which Wendell Truscott could be brought to bay. If it resulted in nothing else, it would at least satisfy a very reasonable curiosity to know what manner of man had played so large and so disastrous a part in the family history.

IV.

Stella had no difficulty in finding the place, a large, new building on a corner of the principal street in the heart of the city. The offices of the Truscott Refining Company were located on the eighth floor of the El Dorado, a modern steel-frame structure towering to the sky as if in defiance of earthly metes and bounds, and housing the population of a small town upon a superficial area no larger than that occupied by a suburban dwelling-house. Stella entered the elevator, which shot skywards rapidly. The sensation of swift upward movement was a novel and disagreeable one. Stella put her hand involuntarily against the side of the car to support herself, and felt a pronounced sense of relief when the car stopped to let her out.

"Eighth floor! Out here, please, lady," said the elevator man. "Number 27, to the right, at the end of the hall."

When Stella had stepped out, he slid the door into place by pulling a lever, and continued his upward flight.

Stella stood in the hall a moment until she had got her bearings. Then she walked along the hall toward the office designated. She could see the number in large gilt letters on the transom over the entrance, and the name of the company on the glazed upper half of the door itself. She had never been in so fine a building. The floor on which she walked was of mosaic, the walls of the passage were wainscoted in white marble and painted in arabesque designs. The wood work was of polished oak with bronze fittings.

Stella knocked at the door somewhat timidly. It was opened by a lad of about fourteen, who seemed surprised at the formality of a knock at the outer door to a business office. He was evidently impressed by Stella's appearance, for when he had glanced at her a somewhat impudent expression gave way to one of greater deference.

"Walk in, ma'am," he said, and added, when she had entered, "Whom did you wish to see?"

"Mr. Truscott. Is he in?" she asked.

"No, ma'am, he's stepped out for a few minutes, but he'll be back right away. Did you want to see him on business?"

"Yes."

"Then you might wait. Just step in here and sit down."

He led the way into an adjoining room, and set a chair for her.

"That's Mr. Truscott's private office," he said, pointing to a room beyond, "and he'll prob'ly pass through here to reach it. He'll be in very soon. Perhaps you'd like to look at the mornin' paper?" he added, bringing it to her. "There's a very interestin' piece in it about a horrible murder and suicide."

Stella thanked him, and let the paper lie on her lap, while she glanced about her. From her seat she could see at a glance the plan of the office, or suite of offices. The room into which she had been shown opened to the right of the one she had entered from the hall. To her left as she went into the second room lay the private office indicated by the boy. These three rooms were at the north side of the west end of the floor, and formed, as it were, three fourths of a square. The other quarter constituted part of a long room occupying the remainder of one side of the eighth floor.

The entrance hall contained a washstand, a table and some chairs. In the room where Stella sat were a filing case, a letter press, a typewriter cabinet, and a green-topped office table. Through the open door to the private office she saw that it was furnished in a style of substantial elegance. She remembered, faintly, having visited her father's office once, when a very little girl; but its furnishings had been vastly simpler than these. The floor had been bare, whereas this was covered with a thick Persian rug. Her father's desk had been an upright affair of black walnut. The one here was a massive roll-top structure of mahogany. A clothes-press stood in one corner. There were several large photographs hanging on the wall, framed in broad frames of plain varnished oak, representing, as she afterward learned, various departments of the company's works. On the side of the private office opposite the main counting-room a chimney, with a grate and a mantel, which extended forward into the room a couple of feet; and just beyond this stood an article of furniture at the sight of which her heart gave a great bound. It was a huge iron safe, and on the front, in gilt letters tarnished by time, she read her father's name,

"Henry P. Merwin." How, she wondered, had this man been able to endure, for all these years, the mute reproach of that name, staring him in the face? Once, when a child, Stella, in a fit of childish petulance, had wounded the feeling of a playmate. She had afterwards repented of it, but the memory of the incident clung to her, and even now she never heard the girl's name without an involuntary pang of shame and regret. Surely this man must be devoid of conscience and incapable of remorse, or this constant reminder of the past must have been unbearable.

When the office boy, after ushering Stella into the second room, returned to his place in the outer office, he was summoned to the counting-room by the head bookkeeper, who stood at his desk, holding a pen between his fingers, as he glanced keenly at the boy.

"Who is that, Johnnie?" he asked sharply.

"It's a lady, sir, to see Mr. Truscott."

"Is it the stenographer we sent for?"

"I guess not, sir. Looks like a lady off the avenoo."

"Did she state her business?"

"No, sir. Shall I ask her?"

"No. Drop these letters in the mail chute."

Johnnie took the letters away. The bookkeeper glanced at a little mirror by the window near his desk, adjusted his necktie, threw a swift look along the counting room to see that his subordinates were at work, and then sauntered with a somewhat mincing step into the room where Stella sat waiting. She rose as he entered, and asked, rather constrainedly:

"Is this Mr. Truscott?"

"No," he said, "I'm Mr. Ross, the head bookkeeper. Was your business with Mr. Truscott personal, or is it something I can attend to?"

There was a suavity and deference in the bookkeeper's voice that inspired confidence, and put Stella somewhat more at her ease.

"I suppose I'll have to see him personally," she replied. "I'm the stenographer sent from Mrs. Paxton's. She gave me a letter—"

"Oh, I see," said the bookkeeper, with a slight falling off in deference, as he took the letter and gave Stella a sweeping glance at which she felt her cheek burn just a trifle. "I thought you were a lady who had called to see him on some other matter. Have you had any experience in office work?"

"No actual office experience," she said, slightly apprehensive, "but I think I understand about what the work is, and I have had a good deal of general practice."

The bookkeeper looked compassionate, and shook his head doubtfully.

"I hope you'll suit him," he said, "but you'll find him rather a hard man to get along with. He's had five stenographers within the year, and has just discharged the last one, who was a rapid and accurate man."

Stella's face betrayed so much dismay at this announcement that he smiled somewhat reassuringly, and explained:

"The stenographer wasn't trustworthy. We couldn't depend on his being here when wanted, and so we had to let him go. We have advertised for another, but good male stenographers are scarce,—the women have almost monopolized the business,—and if you suit Mr. Truscott, and he can't find a good man, you may get the place permanently; that is, if you care for it, of course."

"Thank you," replied Stella, "but I shall probably only stay to-day."

"There's no telling," said the bookkeeper. "In the meantime," he added, with what was intended for a meaning smile, but barely escaped being an offensive smirk, "if I can help you in any way, or say a good word for you I shall be glad to do so."

"You are very kind," said Stella, somewhat drily. She thought the bookkeeper's offers of assistance premature, to say the least, and his manner rather familiar for so short an acquaintance. But before anything more could be said by either, Mr. Truscott entered the office.

As Wendell Truscott came into the room a wave of emotion swept over Stella. This then, was the man whose name was to her the synonym of baseness and treachery. His dark complexion, and stern, not to say heavy features, his rugged, loosely-knit frame, were quite consistent with her conception of his character; and the scar on his lower lip was so much in keeping with the whole that Stella remarked it scarcely more than one would the horns and hoofs in a portrait of the enemy of mankind.

"Mr. Truscott," said Ross, "this is Miss Smith, the stenographer who has come to write your letters."

Mr. Truscott shot a casual glance at Stella, and nodded somewhat stiffly.

"Oh, yes," he said with curtness, "my stenographer isn't here this morning, and I have a lot of letters to answer. Come right into my private office. Mr. Ross will arrange a place for you and we'll start right in."

Mr. Ross, with some falling off of importance, drew out a small table that stood close to the wall, and placed in front of it a straight-backed chair. Stella removed her hat, placed it on the typewriter cabinet in the other room, and then, with some slight trepidation, seated herself at the table.

Mr. Truscott took up the top letter of the pile and dictated an answer. Fortunately for Stella, he did not speak rapidly, and hesitated now and then for a suitable word. This gave her time to get all he said, and to write it with such care that she could read her notes without difficulty. When he had dictated half a dozen letters, he went out in response to a telephone call, saying that he would return in half an hour and proceed with the dictation.

During his absence Stella transcribed the letters on the typewriter. It happened to be the kind of machine she had learned to operate, and was in fairly good order, so that she found the work easy. As she wrote out the letters, she noted, more closely than when taking them, the brusque and peremptory tone of some, in which the writer's disposition was apparent. There was one especially, in reply to a letter from a former employé who had applied for reinstatement, that to Stella seemed particularly cruel. The man had made his plea on the ground that he had a family to support, that his wife was an invalid, and his children too young to care for themselves.

"You have yourself to thank," ran the answer, "for your discharge from our employment. You had fair warning. If we do not enforce the rules of the establishment, discipline will soon cease. If one employé is permitted to come at any hour he pleases, the rest will naturally follow suit. As for your family, I am of course sorry for them, but as the corporation is not a charitable institution, we cannot take such matters into account in determining questions of business management. Our decision in your case was final and cannot be reconsidered."

Stella's blood boiled as she wrote these words; they were such as she might have expected from a man of Wendell Truscott's past. The man who could ruin his benefactor in cold blood, could hardly be expected to show mercy to a subordinate.

Mr. Truscott had not yet returned when Stella had transcribed the last letter. As she read her work over carefully to see if there were any mistakes, she was struck by the clearness of what had been dictated, and the directness and bluntness with which it was stated. Stella surmised that this bluntness was due to a lack of the polish of education, and that it was of a piece with his demeanor. It was of course unreasonable to expect delicacy of speech or thought from one who to a low origin joined a nature so lacking in the feelings and principles that underlie all true refinement. Such a man might possess energy and enterprise, and, by virtue of craft or force, acquire wealth and the sort of position mere wealth can purchase, without ever becoming a gentleman in even the superficial meaning of the word.

It was a very short time in which to reach a conclusion. But Stella prided herself on being a keen reader of character, and had an abiding faith in the boasted intuition of her sex. She had often verified her off-hand impressions by subsequent observation, and had seldom known them to fail. She was sure, after this first hour, that Wendell Truscott was capable of all her mother had charged him with, and that the remainder of her brief sojourn in his office would only confirm her in this belief.

When Mr. Truscott returned, after the lapse of an hour, he read over the letters without comment, signed them, signalled Johnnie and handed, or as it seemed to Stella, who saw him through the open door, threw them at the boy and ordered him to send in the stenographer. When Stella went in, he resumed his dictation without having addressed a single word to her beforehand. The dictation proceeded a little more rapidly than at the former sitting, but her experience with the first batch of letters had given Stella confidence in her skill. Once she asked him to repeat a sentence. He looked slightly surprised, and frowned in an abstracted sort of way, but repeated the sentence, so far as Stella could remember, in exactly the same language as before. In after times she often remarked the exactness of his memory—it seemed a well-ordered storehouse of facts, on which he could draw at a moment's notice, as he might chance to need them. He dictated to her until twelve o'clock, when he touched the button and handed to Johnnie the batch of answered letters.

"File these," he said to the boy; then, turning to Stella, "That's all."

She took her note-book into the stenographer's room, and had sat down at the typewriter, when she noticed the clerks in the counting room putting on their coats and hats and moving toward the outer door.

"Dinner-time, Miss Smith," said Johnnie, sticking his head into her room.

While she hesitated whether to stop or not, with her work unfinished, the bookkeeper, Ross, came in from the counting-room and approached her with the combination of swagger and slyness that seemed to characterize him.

"We stop an hour at twelve for lunch," he said.

"Perhaps Mr. Truscott wants these letters now," she suggested.

"Oh, no," answered Ross, "he'll go out in a minute, and won't get back until two, and it will be quite time enough, if you have them done by then. If there's any information you want, or anything you don't understand, just call on *me*, and I'll explain it. Sometimes, you know, when one starts in at a new thing, one may have it all right and yet not know it, and it's much more satisfactory to be sure about it. If you are doubtful about any letter, just let me read it over, and I can tell you whether it is correct or not."

"Thank you," said Stella, who had risen and was putting on her hat, "if I need help I shall not hesitate to ask for it."

She secretly decided, however, that Mr. Ross was entirely too kind—much kinder than the circumstances called for—and that she would ask no favors of him during the few hours of her stay in the office. It was not exactly what he said, nor

was it just the way in which he said it, that she objected to,—
but a sort of oily officiousness, a compound of self-conceit, of
patronizing condescension and suppressed admiration, that
jarred upon Miss Merwin's nerves. She was as certain that
Ross was a sneak and thought himself a lady-killer, as she was
that Truscott was a heartless tyrant. Of the two she would have
preferred the master to the servant, if perchance she had
meant to work in the office permanently,—one respects the
lion more than the jackal, even though both are beasts of prey.
While she would not have permitted herself to be consciously
prejudiced against Truscott, and simply wished to know what
manner of man he seemed, the facts known by her in advance
had of course prepared her mind for the impression she had
received. If she had found him different, she might have
thought her mother possibly mistaken in regard to his character and conduct. But, so far at least, her mother's conviction
had been borne out by her own observation. On the other
hand, her feeling toward Ross was entirely instinctive. Her
comparison of the two men was equally involuntary.

Before leaving the office she called up Mrs. Paxton by telephone, and arranged to join her at lunch at a nearby restaurant. They were lucky enough to get a small table to themselves,
and after the waiter had taken their orders Mrs. Paxton
inquired about the morning's work.

"Well, Stella," she asked, "how did you get along?"

"Very well, indeed—much better than I had expected.
I took fifteen or twenty letters and wrote half-a-dozen of
them, and there were no complaints, and none of them had
to be rewritten."

"I'm *so* glad you could do it. I always believed in you, Stella. Were the gentlemen nice? Whose dictation did you take?"

"Mr. Truscott's."

"What do you think of him?"

"I think he's horrid."

"Did you meet Mr. Ross, the head bookkeeper?"

"Yes."

"How do you like him?"

"He gives me a creepy feeling, like a mouse or a toad."

"Oh, Stella, I'm shocked at you! I know Mr. Ross quite well; we used to board at the same boarding-house, and he was very polite and kind to the ladies. His wife is a fine woman, but very much of an invalid. She is from my native town and is spending the Summer at home with her parents. You must think well of Mr. Ross, for he sent us the job."

"I won't have much time to learn to like him," said Stella, "if I go home on the four o'clock train this afternoon."

"Are you going? What shall I do?"

"Send Miss Smith to relieve me when I have finished the letters I haven't yet written."

"Oh, dear! I'm afraid they won't like it! Gentlemen don't care to change stenographers, especially during the same day—they say it's like swapping horses while crossing a stream. Miss Smith hasn't finished with Mr. Bushnell yet, either. I'll tell you, Stella!—telegraph your mother, or send a special delivery letter, that you're going to stay all night with me. Then you can finish the day at Mr. Truscott's, and we can go to the theater to-night, and see Bernhardt in *La Tosca*; I did some copying for the press agent and he gave me a couple of tickets, over and above my bill. You can translate the French of the play for me."

"Oh, thank you, Mrs. Paxton, I'll think if over, and I'll do this much now—I'll write mamma that if I don't come up to-night it will be because I'm going to stay with you. Then if I get through in time, or Miss Smith relieves me, I can go home; otherwise I'll stay."

When they had finished their salad and cup of coffee, she went up to Mrs. Paxton's office and wrote a brief note to her mother. She said simply that she was helping Mrs. Paxton in an emergency and might not get through in time for the afternoon train, in which event she would stay until next day. She did not mention Mr. Truscott's name, for she wished to reserve her experiences in his office until she could speak of them at length, and until her impressions had been modified or confirmed by her observations of the afternoon.

V.

Stella was at her desk a few minutes before one. The clerks were all on time. Some of them were just on the hour, and these looked relieved when they glanced up at the clock. Stella supposed their apprehension due to the rigid discipline of the office. She almost shuddered to think that some boy with a widowed mother to support, or some poor man with an invalid wife, might be thrown upon the world at scarcely a moment's notice, because a clock was slow, or a street-car late, or some accident or unforeseen occurrence had delayed him a few minutes beyond the stated hour for beginning work. Perhaps even the stenographer whose place she was taking might have been the innocent victim, for some such reason, of this soul-crushing tyranny,—what Mr. Ross had said about her employer was clearly open to such a construction. When Johnnie next looked into the room she put a question to him.

"Why did the last stenographer leave?"

"Fired," said Johnnie laconically.

"Why?" she inquired.

Johnnie raised his hand to a point about six inches in front of his mouth, and threw his head back suddenly, letting his hand go up so as to retain its relative position to the mouth. Then he hiccoughed and retired with unsteady footsteps to a chair.

She understood this pantomime perfectly. The poor man had been ill, perhaps intoxicated. But no mercy had been shown him, no allowance made for inherited weakness or exceptional temptation, no attention given to promises of amendment. He had been late half an hour, or absent half a day, and had lost his place because, forsooth, the office was not a reformatory, or a hospital, or a "charitable institution." If this was business, then she would have none of it.

She began on the letters and had finished most of them before Mr. Truscott came in. He threw his hat to Johnnie, and passed through Stella's room, without noticing her, into his own office. Johnnie gathered up the letters already typewritten and carried them in to him, and when they were signed copied them in a tissue letter-book on the copying-press, and then brought them back to Stella to be enclosed and addressed. By this time Stella had written the remainder of the letters; and while Mr. Truscott read and signed these, she addressed envelopes for them all. When the last one was signed and enclosed, Johnnie took them out to the mail-chute in the hall, and for a few minutes Stella was left with nothing to do.

Her eyes wandered toward the main office, where some of the clerks were making entries in long canvas-covered books. Others were sorting yellow tissue-paper copies of invoices, others checking up way-bills of railroad and transportation companies. Mr. Ross was at work on a very large ledger, so large that it almost covered the top of his desk. She noticed, however, that he found time, to glance now and then at the little mirror near by, and to turn up the ends of his mustache and adjust his neck-tie. Several times she caught his eyes directed toward her, the last time so steadily that she turned her head.

Through the open door of the private office she could see Mr. Truscott opening the letters that had come by the latest mail delivery. His face was clearly outlined against the window beyond him, and there came before the girl's mind the greatest treasure of her home—a portrait of her father, done in oil by a struggling artist whom he had wished to encourage—he had been fond of helping young men,—too fond, Stella thought,—but who had since attained celebrity. She could not resist contrasting her father's kindly features with Truscott's harsh and saturnine profile.

"Hyperion to a satyr," she murmured.

Just then the electric annunciator by her side sounded twice. She was looking around in uncertainty, when Johnnie thrust his head into the doorway.

"That's for you, Miss Smith," he said. "Once for me, twice for the stenographer, and three times for Mr. Ross."

Stella took her note-book and went into Mr. Truscott's room.

"I want to dictate a contract," he said, looking out of the window.

He commenced the dictation, and went on with it much as he had with the letters. Presently he rose, and began to pace the floor as he dictated. Stella wished he would sit still, instead of striding back and forth in that nervous way, like a caged lion. He must know that she could not hear him distinctly when he was walking away from her; but of course he could hardly be expected to care for the convenience of a subordinate. By-and-by he stopped when at the other end of his promenade and lit a cigar. He made several turns, his voice even more indistinct because of the obstruction in his mouth. Stella said nothing, until the smoke, to which she was unaccustomed, threw her into a violent fit of coughing.

Mr. Truscott looked at her, for the first time during the afternoon, so far as she had observed.

"Perhaps you don't like smoke?" he said.

"I detest it," she answered.

"Oh, I beg pardon," he said drily, and threw the cigar into the grate. He continued the dictation, with occasional interruptions, until five o'clock. As Stella rose, after he had finished, she saw the clerks in the main office closing their books and preparing to go home.

"Write that out in the morning," said Mr. Truscott. "I shall want it by ten o'clock."

Stella had quite made up her mind not to come back next day under any circumstances. She had seen enough of Wendell Truscott to verify her mother's belief and her own first impressions. The man was without heart, without manners, and, she felt with some humiliation, without taste. He had not addressed twenty words to her during the day, and had noticed her no more than had she been a piece of furniture. Stella was not unused to admiration, and knew that her appearance and carriage were striking; but she might as well have been any one of a hundred dowdy shop-girls whom she met on the street, for any impression she had made upon that block of granite. Nevertheless, in spite of her determination, for some reason she did not make any reply, but walked somewhat stiffly out with her note-book and pen. She could easily write the contract at Mrs. Paxton's in the morning, and deliver it by ten o'clock. In the meantime, the real Miss Smith could report at the office at eight o'clock, which she had been informed was the regular hour for beginning the day's work.

Johnnie brought her hat, an unusual condescension for Johnnie to make to any employé, and bade her good night as she went out.

"Fine girl, Johnnie," said one of the clerks who remained in the office a few minutes after Stella had gone.

"She's a peach," said Johnnie with decision.

"Wish she'd stay," said the clerk.

"Can if she wants to," said Johnnie. "*He* likes her."

"How do you know?"

"I knows *him*. No cussin,' no tearin' up, no writin' over!"

"Thought he wouldn't have a woman around the office?"

"Never seemed to know she was in the office. Wouldn't need to know whether she was a woman or a man, if he didn't look. *He* talks and *she* writes and that's the end of it. Betcher a box er coffin-nails he'll ask her to stay."

"Done, Johnnie. If I win, I'm a box in. If I lose, I'll only hasten your death,—you're too clever to live long, anyway, Johnnie. You'll die young."

"Might gimme one now, on account," said Johnnie, "for I'm sure to win."

The clerk tossed him a cigarette, which Johnnie lit and puffed with the zest and satisfaction of a connoisseur.

VI.

When Stella and Mrs. Paxton dismounted from the street-car in front of the brilliantly lighted entrance to the theater, a fashionably attired throng were pouring into the lobby and carriages were depositing their freight of ladies and gentlemen in evening dress upon the curbstone, whence they passed beneath a canopy to the entrance. A policeman was on duty to protect them from too close contact with the vulgar. Bernhardt's appearance for three nights, on her second American tour, was a great event, and society turned out in full force to look at her,—so far as the play was concerned, it might as well have been in pantomime, for anything that all but a few of the audience understood of what was said. As Stella and her friend moved with the crowd along the lobby, Mrs. Paxton pointed out several well-known people of local prominence.

"That's Mr. Jewitt, the multi-millionaire. If he should look this way he'd speak to me. I worked in his office when I first began to earn my own living, and I am sure he hasn't forgotten me."

Just then the great man turned his head in their direction and smiled and nodded blandly, Stella could not tell, of course, whether to them or to someone else in the lobby. Mrs. Paxton gave an answering smile and moved as if to come nearer to him. But he looked the other way and before she could reach him, was lost in the crowd.

"He's an awfully nice man," she said, "and as charitable as he is rich. He has founded a hospital and endowed a dozen colleges. He has given the city a park. He spends millions for charity, and employs a man on a salary to investigate cases that are brought to his attention.

"That's Professor Bowles,"—indicating a tall man with long white hair and beard—" 'the distinguished lecturer on comparative religions, theosophy and kindred topics.' That's from his letterhead—we do his correspondence in the office. He is a very learned man and knows all about the secret history and occult meaning of the Sphinx and the pyramids. That man has forgotten more than most people ever knew."

"Oh, yes," said Stella, "I have heard him lecture in our town." She did not add, as she might have done, that, from what she had heard of the professor, he had probably forgotten all that was worth knowing, and had retained only the odds and ends of vanished faiths and discredited speculations.

Mrs. Paxton pointed out the mayor, who looked for all the world like a successful brewer; the lady minister of a Universalist church, at whom Stella, in spite of her own enlightened views, looked with something of repulsion. The reverend lady, no longer young, wore a close-fitting dress of some dark stuff, with a vest-front and a standing collar in what Stella thought a rather ludicrous imitation of the clerical garb. A woman preacher of religion in attendance upon a play written by Sardou and interpreted by Bernhardt, was a combination that Stella's degree of intellectual advancement had not yet prepared her to contemplate without some mental confusion.

They presented their tickets at the door, and soon found themselves in very comfortable seats in the front row of the balcony. The house was filled to overflowing. The display of costumes, of shoulders and of jewels was far beyond anything Stella had ever seen before. For although she had been brought up within thirty miles of Groveland, and had often visited the city and more than once the theater, she had never seen such a house. The eight or ten private boxes of which the theater boasted were all occupied except one or two, with groups in which ladies predominated.

Mrs. Paxton turned her opera glass toward various parts of the house, and as she recognized people of more or less distinction, handed the glass to Stella and pointed them out. Mrs. Paxton seemed to have quite a wide acquaintance, especially among the semi-public people who write letters to the newspapers to promote public charities and further social reforms, most of whom seemed to have had work done in her office at various times, and some of whom she had met at reform gatherings of one kind or another, of which she was a frequent attendant.

By-and-by the orchestra played the music of the opening scene of the third act of *Die Walküre*. Stella was fond of Wagner, and for a quarter of an hour was lost to everything but his magic. Above the rugged mountain-peaks, amid the play of lightning and the thunder of the storm, Stella could see the wild Valkyries on their war-steeds dashing through the ragged clouds to the rescue of Brunnhilde; she could hear their war-like chorus urging mankind to combat, so that they might find among the fallen heroes of earth recruits for the guard of Walhalla. The orchestra was a fine one and well-conducted, and even the hum of conversation in the boxes was swept away by this flood of transcendent harmony. After making one or two remarks which Stella was too absorbed to hear, even Mrs. Paxton relapsed into silence until the last lingering note had died away. A moment later the prompter's bell was heard faintly tinkling in the wings, and the curtain rose upon the scene in the cathedral.

Then for an hour Stella watched the wonderful delineation of character by the great tragedienne. It was on the occasion of Bernhardt's second visit to America. The actress was in the plenitude of her artistic powers, for the display of which the play gave admirable opportunity. Stella could follow the French indifferently well and thought what she took to be the pure Parisian accent of the players very different from the pronunciation she had learned at school. She had read the synopsis of the play, and had the book on her lap before her, with a convenient interlinear translation to help the reader over the hard places. But she scarcely had occasion to look at it, even if there had been light enough to read by, so absorbed was she in the hurried action, and the powerful portrayal of human character and passion. Bernhardt's support, it occurred to her at times, was not as good as it might have been, but the central figure seemed so completely to fill the stage as to radiate energy and feeling to those about her;—while in a sense it dominated and dwarfed them, yet it seemed at the same time to embrace them and absorb them and make them harmonious parts of one great conception. Some of the audience stared blankly at the stage, evidently lost without the words. But to Stella, by virtue perhaps of the intuition that formed so strong an element of her character, events unrolled themselves in natural sequence, and the incidents of the play seemed as clear as if she had understood every word. She did not like the story of the play; much of it was repugnant to her pure, fresh mind. But the acting fascinated her. She felt a vague sense of power stirring within her—a feeling that she too could become a great actress, or write a great play, or in some way achieve renown.

At the end of the first act Stella returned from the land of romance to the world of reality. Mrs. Paxton indulged in some comments on the play and began again her survey of the audience, which had been slightly augmented by arrivals during the act. In a few moments she handed her glass to Stella, who directed it toward one of the lower tier of boxes almost opposite where they sat. When she had looked for a moment at the occupants she returned the glass to Mrs. Paxton.

"There is Mr. Truscott" she said, "the gentleman nearest the stage, in the second box from the front."

"Oh, yes," said Mrs. Paxton when she had scanned the party, "I've seen him before, although I never knew who he was. I quite agree with you that he doesn't look like an agreeable man. But who is the lady he is sitting by? It seems to me I've seen her before. Oh, yes! I recognize her now. It's Miss Wedderburn, president of the Monthly Club. I remember we wrote some letters for her three or four years ago. She's very rich, lives on Oakwood Avenue, and is a leader in literary and musical circles. She's not as young as she used to be, but she's very swell. Your Mr. Truscott must be quite fond of music, I often see his name among the patrons of concerts and other musical events."

"I should never have guessed it," returned Stella. "The thought of him in connection with music would suggest a dancing bear more than anything else."

The second musical number was a familiar Strauss waltz, and its soothing strains served as a pleasant corrective of the emotional stress evoked by the play. Stella looked long and carefully at the lady in company with Wendell Truscott, not from any special interest in either, but merely because they were the only people whose names she knew, and because she wondered, in a vaguely speculative way, what manner of woman it was who could find pleasure in such companionship. The lady, she surmised, must be at least thirty-five; she seemed younger, but Stella knew her sex well enough to know that when a woman has passed thirty, she makes herself look five years younger, if possible, and a woman of Miss Wedderburn's means and position would undoubtedly have command of all the arts of the toilet. She was not of that type of unmarried women who grow thin after the flight of youth, but one of those who in pleasant surroundings, with agreeable occupations, ripen gradually to maturity and then gracefully shade off into old age. She had an intellectual forehead and wore her hair so as to render this fact apparent. Her gown was cut to reveal a superb neck and shoulders, and her eyes sparkled with subdued vivacity as she conversed, now with Mr. Truscott and now with some other one of their party. She wore diamonds in her ears, and upon her corsage a splendid brooch, the light from which flashed in close juxtaposition to a superb bunch of Maréchal Niel roses. Stella was not of an envious disposition, but as she saw this woman seated by Wendell Truscott, she could not avoid the reflection that had it not been for the latter's baseness, *she* might have been seated in a box, and might have worn diamonds that would have set off her youthful beauty to even greater advantage than they decorated the maturer charms of Miss Wedderburn. Nevertheless she found some small compensation in the thought that even then she would not have needed them as much as did the other woman.

The curtain rose and again the great actress drew on the resources of her art. The action was even more rapid than in the first act; the plot thickened, and the interest became more intense. But the continuity of Stella's attention had been broken by the intrusion of a new idea, and every now and then she found her eyes straying from the scene upon the stage to the couple in the second box from the front. They were seated in the rear of the box, and she could not watch the play of their countenances so well as when the lights had been turned up, but she could see that they too were not all attention to the stage, but were from time to time engaged in conversation.

The third and most thrilling act riveted Stella's attention, and the fourth held it; and it was not until the curtain fell that she glanced again, as she rose to go, at the box occupied by Miss Wedderburn and Truscott. Truscott was laying a fleecy opera cloak upon Miss Wedderburn's gleaming shoulders. Stella saw him smile, and almost shuddered at the sinister expression of the side of his face turned toward her. The ugly scar upon his lip seemed to spread until it dominated and lent character to the whole countenance. In this instance the face was indeed the index of the soul.

She accompanied Mrs. Paxton home and spent the night with her. Mrs. Paxton was fond of talking, and loved an intelligent auditor. Stella was in a pensive mood, and not a little tired. Her business experience of the day—her contact with the man who had ruined her father—the excitement of the play—had given unaccustomed exercise to her emotions, and ere long she fell asleep, with Mrs. Paxton's cheerful and high-pitched voice still sounding in her ears.

VII.

When Stella and her friend reached the latter's office in the morning they found a note from Miss Smith, to the effect that she was ill and would be unable to report for duty during the day.

"I don't know what in the world I shall do, Stella," said Mrs. Paxton despairingly. "Every one of my girls is busy, and I don't know where to turn for another. *Please* stay and help me out until noon! Something may turn up by that time. It will give you an opportunity to get your contract written. I shall charge a good price for your services, and it will be interesting to be able to say that you once earned some money at your shorthand."

"Oh, dear, no, Mrs. Paxton, I'm only doing it to oblige you! I wouldn't touch a cent of Mr. Truscott's money."

"Money is money, my dear Stella. We call it 'filthy lucre'; but it has the unique faculty of self-purification. It is like a king—it can do no wrong. The law recognizes its impeccability—I've learned enough of law in my business to know that you cannot follow stolen money, after it has once passed from the thief to an innocent party who gave value for it. Never sneer at money, Stella, and get all that you can honestly. I wouldn't dream of letting you work for me for nothing!"

So Stella, to oblige her friend, went back to the Truscott Refining Company's office to remain until noon. When she left the elevator a half-dozen or more young men and women got off at the same floor, and as she entered the outer door of the office they were close behind her. In the outer office were seated a number of young people and, in the room where she worked, half a dozen others. As she took her seat at the type-writer a new batch evidently appeared at the door, for she heard Johnnie addressing them in a somewhat dictatorial tone.

"Youse'll have to wait out in the hall," he was saying, "until some of these others come out. There ain't no more room inside. Mr. Truscott won't be down till ten o'clock nohow."

This announcement was repeated from time to time, and when Stella had occasion to go out into the hall, about an hour later, she saw a dozen or more standing *en queue* along the hall. When she came in Johnnie beckoned her from the private office, to which he had temporarily retreated in order to main-tain the dignified reserve befitting an employé of the company in dealing with those who did not enjoy that distinction.

"See all them slobs?" he said in a hoarse whisper. "They're all lookin' for your job. But Mr. Truscott won't have none of 'em!"

"I should think he could find a good stenographer among so many," said Stella, scanning the gathering with greater interest.

"He won't have none of 'em," said Johnnie, positively. "They ain't his style. He likes *you*."

"He can't have me, Johnnie, for I'm going away at noon."

"Oh, *don't* go, Miss Smith! I like a lady like you round a place. These cheap-lookin' guys give me a pain. Look at them letters!" he said, pointing to a large heap of unopened envelopes.

While they stood talking, the postman came in with still another lot, which swelled the heap alarmingly. Stella felt somewhat apprehensive at the thought that she might be expected to write answers to them all. Her position for the morning would evidently be no sinecure.

"Them's nearly all letters from typewriters," confided the boy; "but that ain't a circumstance to the pile he got when he advertised before. There was two waste-baskets full."

Stella returned to her desk and proceeded with her contract. She noticed now and then the waiting young men and girls eyeing her, some of them curiously, as if wondering why she were going to give up the place; some enviously, as if they thought she might have got ahead of them over night; some disdainfully, from the height, Stella supposed, of their superior skill. She had just finished the contract when the clock in the main office pointed to ten.

A moment later Mr. Truscott came in. He merely glanced at the waiting throng, passed into his private office, and as he sat down touched the button for Johnnie.

"Tell Mr. Ross to come here. Mr. Ross," he said, when that functionary had appeared, "who are all these people?"

"They have come in answer to the advertisement, sir."

"Show me the advertisement!"

Mr. Ross produced a morning paper. "There it is, sir," he said—

"Wanted, an experienced male stenographer, of good habits. Address, by letter, stating experience and giving reference, The Truscott Refining Company, 27 El Dorado Building."

"That is quite specific. Send all those people away."

Mr. Ross dismissed those who were waiting. Some looked disappointed, others lingered hopefully; but they were all sent away with the statement that no applications would receive any attention whatever unless in writing. One rather handsome, very fair girl, with a fine figure, a bold face, and fluffy hair, almost insisted on seeing Mr. Truscott.

"I'm sure if he'd talk to me a moment he'd employ me," she said. "A personal interview would be much more satisfactory than writing a stupid letter. *Do* see if you can't get him to see me."

"I'll see what I can do," said Ross, "if I can help you I will."

He went into the private office, and Stella heard him ask Mr. Truscott some question about the office business, after which he returned to the blonde young woman.

"I'm sorry," he said, "but you'll have to write. If you'll drop me a line at the same time"—Stella heard him add, though in a lowered tone, "—giving me your name and address, perhaps I can say a good word for you."

"Oh, thank you," said the young woman eagerly. "You're too good for anything. I'd like the job first-rate," she added, sweeping a look from her long lashes over the room of young men at work in the outer office.

Stella looked at her with something like disgust, and felt for a moment as though the young woman were seeking to usurp her place. She could almost stay, to keep such a creature out. Surely there must be among the numerous applicants some modest and worthy young woman deserving of preference over this loud, aggressive and over-dressed person. She felt glad that she was not compelled by necessity to pursue a calling in which she would come into competition with people of that stamp.

Before Mr. Truscott called her she was summoned to the telephone. Mrs. Paxton had rung her up.

"Whom do you suppose I have just been talking to?" asked her friend.

"I could never guess. Who was it?"

"Your mother!"

"Well, that *is* a surprise! When did she come down?"

"She isn't in town. She called up the office by the long distance, from Cloverdale, and we had quite a talk. I have her consent to persuade you to stay over and help me out until Miss Smith gets well. I'll meet you at lunch, at the same place."

Stella had scarcely resumed her seat before the "buzzer" sounded twice and she went into Mr. Truscott's office.

"Miss—Jones," he said without looking at her, "I have divided this stack of letters into two piles. These in this larger pile I suspect are applicants for the position of stenographer. I wish you would take this paper-knife and open them all, sometime during the day, as you find opportunity. Those that are not well written or correctly spelled, throw into the wastebasket. If there are any that seem to suggest glimmerings of intelligence, lay them aside and hand them to me when you have gone through the lot."

She took the letters to her desk and began to open them. Mr. Truscott looked through the rest of the morning mail and soon called her to take dictation. He gave her letters enough to occupy her until well along in the afternoon. She worked at the typewriter steadily until the noon hour, when she went out to luncheon.

"Your mother agrees with me, Stella," said Mrs. Paxton when they were comfortably seated, "that a little practical experience will be an excellent thing for you, and will put you in a position to decide whether or not you would care for a business career. I think it really degrading for a woman, equipped by nature and training to accomplish something serious in the world's work, to rush off, before she has really acquired a firm grasp of her implements or a clear conception of her powers, and marry, as such women almost always do— some inferior man, who spoils what might otherwise be a well-rounded career. For clever women always marry sticks."

"Perhaps the men merely suffer from comparison," returned Stella. "But at any rate, Mrs. Paxton, some women must marry and do the housework and rear the children."

"There'll always be enough for such uses," rejoined Mrs. Paxton. "But minds like yours are built for nobler ends. Your mother says she may come to town toward the end of the week, and that in the meantime I am to stand to you *in loco parentis*; you are to stay with me and obey my instructions until she resumes her authority. Now, will you be good!"

When Stella had written the day's letters, she again attacked the pile of applications, and in the course of the afternoon read through them all. The most were poorly written, some with the pen and others upon the typewriter. Even more were badly spelled, and she wondered what conception the writers could have of what was required in a business office. The advertisement to which these letters were responses had called for a male stenographer. Three-fourths of the answers were from young women—she was sure they were young, most of them, because of the quality of their productions. They put forth various and novel reasons why they should be employed. One had an invalid mother to support, another a bedridden father. Another was the eldest of ten children, all of whom, apparently, were dependent upon her for support. A third was a young widow. One had been on the stage;—Stella could scarcely imagine why this fact should be put forward as a qualification for the position of stenographer. Still another had seen better days, and was sure that she could diffuse an atmosphere of refinement about the office that would have a good moral effect upon the male clerks there employed. Some of the applications betrayed an absolutely hopeless ignorance, both of grammar and of the world. Stella shrunk from her task; she wished that her employer had himself assumed the responsibility of crushing the hopes of these aspiring hearts. It was with a pang of regret that she threw into the waste-basket even the worst of them; and she scarcely doubted the estimate Mr. Truscott would make of her own intelligence when he should look over the very generous heap she placed upon his table.

He paid no attention to these letters during the afternoon, but at about half past four o'clock called Stella into his office and dictated business correspondence to her until five, the usual hour for closing.

VIII.

When Wendell Truscott reached his office next morning, he found among the letters on his desk a square envelope, addressed in a feminine hand, and sealed with a monogram seal. He opened it first of all and read the following:

"Dear Wendell—

"Can you come up to dinner at seven Saturday evening? It will be very informal and the company will be small—mostly members of the family.

"Sincerely yours,
"Matilda Wedderburn."

Mr. Truscott read the letter and put it in the inside breast-pocket of his coat. Then he glanced through the remainder of the morning mail, made memoranda on some of the letters, threw several into the waste-basket, and filed others away.

Wendell Truscott had known Matilda Wedderburn for a number of years. He had met her first, indeed, at the Merwin residence, at a time when he was a poor clerk, and only enjoyed by his employer's favor the privilege of meeting such a fine flower of culture as Matilda Wedderburn. She was of an old family, as American families go; indeed her pedigree dated back to colonial times and had numbered persons of distinction in almost every generation. She was rich in larger measure than falls to the common lot even among rich people;—not a multi-millionaire, but one of the solidly rich whose wealth consists in brick and stone blocks and government bonds and other gilt-edged securities. Her father had been for many years engaged in extensive business enterprises. He had lived to middle age and had added materially to an already large inherited fortune. Like a wise man, he knew the uncertainty of life, and while yet comparatively young had withdrawn from his business such part of his fortune as he did not need for working capital, and had so invested it as, at his death, to place his only daughter in a financial position that nothing short of an earthquake or a revolution could shake or render insecure.

Miss Wedderburn had been educated in a style befitting her fortune and a really fine mind. She had travelled extensively and spent a number of years in foreign countries, whose tongues, in several instances, she spoke with fluency and correctness. She had a fine library, largely of her own selection, and was well acquainted with its contents. But music was her master passion. One of the first to introduce the Wagner cult into her city, and among the foremost in the United States to sound the praises of the music of the future, she had been several times to Bayreuth to attend the Wagner Festival, and was a personal friend of the composer's widow. In her work as president or secretary of the Monthly Musical Club, she found a congenial outlet for her energy, to which this organization owed its very high place in the musical world. There were few concert singers or instrumentalists of the higher rank who did not receive with eagerness an invitation from the Monthly Club of Groveland, for it invariably meant an appreciative audience and a financial success.

But this field was not wide enough to embrace all of Miss Wedderburn's activities. Of benevolent disposition, she patronized orphan asylums, hospitals and other deserving charities.

A kindergarten bore her name, and the Wedderburn scholarship in one of the best female colleges had helped more than one ambitious young woman to a good education. She did not blazon her small charities to an applauding world, and neither did she advertise the fact that she did not blazon them, for she had none of "the pride that apes humility." As for her public benefactions, she held that a proper example was often conducive to praiseworthy emulation, and so did not hide her light under a bushel. And, with all the active interest she took in these several matters, she never nagged or scolded, but did what she did with such perfect good taste and such unfailing tact, that the pleasure of receiving a favor at her hands was almost as great as the benefit conferred. Even her dogs would rather lick her empty hand than take tidbits from another.

And yet, despite her superiority, or perhaps because of it, Matilda Wedderburn had passed thirty and was still unmarried. For this there were several reasons. She had gone in for the higher culture in earnest, and by the time she had graduated from college her taste for immature young men had vanished. If some one had struck her fancy at this time she would doubtless have married. But the young men who paid her attention were either not up to her intellectual standard, or were open to suspicion as to fortune-hunting, or did not please her personally.

Then she went abroad for several years with her father, who had retired from business, and the life in foreign lands attracted and charmed her. At first she found her pleasure in wandering about old cathedral towns, in climbing the walls of dismantled castles, and in lingering amid the treasures of great art galleries. She visited the fallen temples of Greece, drove over the hills of Rome, stood in the shadow of the pyramids, and guessed at the riddle of the Sphinx. Then she began to appreciate the well-ordered manner of life, prevailing in these older countries,—the careful adjustment of means to comfortable ends in the mere art of living; and when she found time to seek the society in which her wealth and culture fitted her to shine, she was pleased with the old-world system of social intercourse—a hierarchy in which each had his recognized place and value. With all her liberality, Matilda Wedderburn was a born conservative. She liked the deference of common people to their superiors, and she was both able and willing to pay its price. Servility did not seem out of place in countries where people were trained to it, and superiority seemed much more real when it was not questioned.

She was not without the usual swarm of admirers who surround the rich American girl. But, despite her appreciation of the mellow foreign life, she was intensely loyal to her own country and her own people. She could perceive that in some particulars the ripeness of European civilization verged upon decay. She regarded the shortcomings of her own country as the faults of youth. She believed its basic principle, the essential equality of man, to be the true keystone of the arch of liberty; and she deemed it easier to correct the waywardness of youth, easier to heal the growing pains of the republic, than to rejuvenate states fallen into national decrepitude. And even if, as political philosophers were prone to predict, the nation should go to shipwreck on the shoals of democracy, she was convinced that it was nevertheless the finest of ideals, the one cause above all others where failure would be but the harbinger of success. In her high creed,—

> "Never yet
> Share of truth was vainly set
> In the world's wide fallow."

Perhaps it was because she loved her own country so well that Miss Wedderburn had refused a dozen titles. Of French and Italian noblemen we will make no account. An English marquis had tendered her his coronet in vain. An escutcheon quartered with royal arms and dating back to the Norman conquest, had failed to dazzle her. It was related of her that a certain noble earl of ancient lineage, much impressed by her charms of mind and person, had invited her, with her father, to stay at his castle. The noble earl, it was said, had found Miss Wedderburn even more attractive at close quarters than in casual meetings, and had about decided to offer her his hand and all that went with it, including at least the fragment of a generous heart—for the noble earl had lived the life of his kind and was well on toward middle age when, walking in his garden one day he had seen the object of his admiration seated beneath a certain rustic arbor. The earl was well informed concerning Miss Wedderburn's antecedents; in fact, he was a gentleman who made it a point to acquire information on such matters as interested him. He knew, as even Matilda herself did not, that the ancestor from whom she traced her long descent, from the American point of view, had been a servant of one of his own progenitors. In acquiring this information the earl had taken occasion to look over the books of the estate,—they had been preserved for two hundred years or more,—and had learned that this ancestor of Matilda Wedderburn had built the original of the very arbor that formed so beautiful a setting for the picture of womanly grace within it. For a moment the fragment of the noble earl's heart struggled with the robust entirety of his pride of birth, with the result that the proposal he had gone out to make was turned into a graceful inquiry about the lady's health. True, Miss Wedderburn's ancestor had long been dead; the arbor had been many times renewed, but the association of ideas had proved too much for the noble earl's inherited instinct.

This was merely a story; no one ever quoted it to Miss Wedderburn, for obvious reasons. It was quite improbable that the noble earl himself should have told it, for he was as distinguished for courtesy and a high sense of honor, as for his ancient lineage. And yet the story might easily have been true. That Matilda would have accepted the honor of this exalted matrimonial alliance is doubtful. There would have been some attraction in the name, and in the station to which it would have called her; but she had already the entrée to this brilliant circle, and it is safe to say that no fragment of a heart, however superfine the quality, would have satisfied Matilda Wedderburn. She had often said that she would never marry except for love; that she had everything else that women marry for, and that if she never met the man whom she could love, she could quite afford to remain unmarried.

She had known Wendell Truscott for many years. In those early days, when she had seen him, an awkward youth in the parlors of her friend Mrs. Merwin, she had scarcely noticed him. Later on, when he gave promise of becoming a great captain of industry, she had met him in society, and had come in contact with him, after her father's death, in the transaction of some business concerning her property; for she kept track of her own affairs with absolute thoroughness. She had been struck by the clearness with which Wendell Truscott seemed to grasp business propositions, and by the good judgment with which he could forecast the future. He had seemed to her to reach by intuition conclusions that others could only figure out laboriously. His manners were not quite up to her standard, and for a time she had thought them crude and unformed; but time and prosperity and association with the best people, had improved him in these respects until he seemed, to Matilda at least, a model of courtesy. To what extent this opinion was due to partiality for him, or whether his manner toward her was affected by any tenderness of feeling, she did not for a long time consider. When at length she confessed to herself that Wendell Truscott came nearer being her ideal than any man she had ever met, she was yet in doubt whether she had inspired in him a feeling of more than friendship. That he admired her was self-evident; indeed, he had more than once said so, in that non-committal way in which a man of the world can tell a lady any pleasant thing. That he preferred her society to that of other women was equally apparent, for he sought it oftener. And while he had never said a word to her that he might not have said to any other woman—though not with equal truthfulness in every case, Miss Wedderburn flattered herself;—and though she was a woman who believed that she had perfect control of her thoughts and her emotions, there came a time when she hoped that he would say to her what he had never said, so far as she could learn, to any other woman. She had a thorough knowledge of the world, and in a very womanly way and with entire respect for the proprieties, she gave him every opportunity to manifest any such feeling that he might have. She thought, or had begun to think, that she saw signs of what she hoped for; but she was no longer very young, and knew that the wish is often father to the thought. So she built no false hopes, but patiently awaited developments. She felt secure in his friendship; she had a perfect knowledge of his tastes; there was no other woman between them, and she had no fear as to the outcome.

Of late she had come to think the time about ripe for Wendell to declare himself. When they had last been together, which was at the theater to hear Bernhardt in *La Tosca*, he had been more than usually attentive, and she thought that she had detected in his voice a new and more tender note. She felt sure that her instinct had not failed her, and that the next time they met, if the circumstances were favorable, he would speak the words that would make her happy. She determined that the opportunity should not be too long delayed. Hence the note Wendell Truscott had received in his mail on the morning of the third day that Stella Merwin had come to work in his office.

IX.

When Truscott had looked through his correspondence he summoned the stenographer. This time he glanced at Stella and spoke a shade more pleasantly than he had hitherto addressed her.

"Good morning, Miss er-ah-Jones, I"—

"Smith, if you please," said Stella, mustering up a bit of courage. For strangely enough, though she despised and hated the man, she always felt small when she came into his presence. She did not know whether it was the mere sex instinct of subordination, or simply the effect of a virile nature radiating an atmosphere of authority.

"I beg your pardon," he said, "I wish to dictate some letters, Miss Smith."

The janitress who had cleaned the office the evening before had moved Stella's chair from its accustomed place, and as she started toward it, Mr. Truscott rose and brought the chair from the other side of the room.

"Thank you," said Stella, and took her seat, opened her notebook and grasped her pen.

She wondered whether the fact that she had changed her gown from that of the day before, had called his attention to the fact that he was dictating his letters to a woman instead of to a male stenographer inured to smoke and subject to occasional intoxication. Perhaps, she thought, he might, if she remained in the office long enough, perceive that she was a lady, and entitled to the courtesy due to one, unless, indeed, life in an office involved a different standard of manners from that of ordinary social intercourse. If Stella had known of the perfumed note in Wendell Truscott's breast-pocket, she might have found other cause than her own influence to account for his improvement of manner.

Mr. Truscott seemed slightly preoccupied this morning. He dictated his letters even more slowly than heretofore and hesitated oftener for the proper word. Once he waited so long in the middle of a sentence, that Stella almost involuntarily suggested a word.

"Thank you," he said, giving her a keen glance; "that would ordinarily be the proper expression. But this man would not understand it in the right way."

Whereat Stella felt crushed and very meekly wrote what he finally dictated, perceiving that it conveyed the idea exactly and beyond any possibility of misunderstanding.

As Truscott gradually cleared his desk, he reached the pile of letters selected by Stella from the answers to the advertisement, and, while she sat waiting, looked the letters over. As one followed another rapidly into the waste-basket, Stella felt herself sinking lower and lower in his estimation. She held the man, and his character, and his life, in utter detestation. In the abstract, his opinion of her would possess for her no value whatever. And yet she could not prevent the involuntary reflection that, if perchance he should at some time learn her real identity, it would give additional poignancy to any feelings of regret or remorse of which he might be capable, to appreciate the superior quality of one whom he had wronged. If the whirligig of time should ever bring around the hour of her revenge, she thought it would be the sweeter and his punishment the sharper, if he could realize that for a few short days he had been subjected to the clear light of an intelligence able to read his true character in all its odious aspects.

When by this summary process he had reduced the number of the letters about one-half, he settled himself back in his chair and glanced at Stella, who grasped her pen more firmly and leaned slightly toward the table. But the expected dictation did not come, and glancing up a moment later, Stella saw that he was looking toward her—not *at* her, but merely gazing into vacancy, for his eyes wore that introspective look that marks abstraction from one's immediate surroundings. Stella could not decide which was more humiliating—not to be looked at all, or to be looked at without being seen. On the whole she thought the former the less provoking.

"I think I'll not answer these now," he said at length, "there's no hurry about them."

He threw the letters on the table, and picked up the other pile, on which he had made notations.

"I wish you'd answer these letters yourself," he said. "You'll find the addresses in them, and I've made on each a minute of what I wish to say. You've written letters enough now to get the run of my style, and can answer these quite well enough."

Stella took the sheets from his hand and went into her own room. The task was not an agreeable one. His disposition of the letters she had examined had not been encouraging. He would have even a lower opinion of her intelligence when he should have read her answers to the annotated letters. Nevertheless, after transcribing the fresh dictation, she bravely started upon the work of composition.

Mr. Truscott was not quite in his usual business frame of mind this morning, as Stella had surmised. When she had left the room he summoned Ross and discussed with him certain details of the business. Later on, one of the directors called, and was closeted with him for half an hour. After the director's departure, Mr. Truscott opened a drawer in his desk and extracted a handful of letters, several of which he read over thoughtfully before replacing the whole. Having disposed of these business matters, he then drew from his breast-pocket the letter he had received in the morning mail, re-read it thoughtfully, placed it on the desk before him, and sat thinking for five minutes,—

"My dear Matilda:-

"I shall be glad to come tomorrow night. I have felt my loneliness more of late than ever before. I trust you will give me an opportunity to ask a question that has long been upon my mind, and that you will not refuse me the answer I desire above all things.

"Faithfully yours,
"Wendell Truscott."

Having blotted and folded the letter, he looked in a pigeon-hole for an envelope of suitable size to enclose it. Not finding one, he touched the button for Johnnie, and despatched him to a neighboring stationer's for a box of envelopes.

While Johnnie was gone upon this errand Truscott sat waiting and thinking.

He had known Matilda Wedderburn since she first came out, years before, in all the glory of a wealthy debutante, and had gazed from a respectful distance at this dazzling beauty, around whom swarmed men that scarcely spoke to him when they met him. He had seen the bud unfold into the perfect flower. For a long time their paths had not run close together, and only in more recent years, since his position in the industrial and social world had become firmly established, had he met her on a footing of more than conventional equality. They had been thrown much together, at first by chance, and more recently from choice. Some contraries attract, and there were many respects in which Matilda Wedderburn was the antithesis of Wendell Truscott. For instance, he made large sums of money, but apparently gave very little of it away, using it to swell the already large capital employed in his business. He had always, however, responded promptly and cheerfully to any demands of the kind made by Miss Wedderburn or at her instance. He was taciturn, while she was a ready conversationalist and seemed always to say the right thing at just the right moment. She was musical, while to him Verdi was tiresome, and Wagner's most sublime harmonies a mere jumble of discordant sounds. Miss Wedderburn had once attempted to teach him the bass to a popular negro melody that she thought within his musical comprehension, but the result had discouraged any future efforts in that direction. He realized that his standards of taste in some respects were not quite hers, yet the bond of sympathy between them had grown stronger and stronger. Indeed he had for several years meant to marry Matilda Wedderburn, as soon as he could find time. The wedding of such a woman, he imagined, would be regarded as a great social function, to be celebrated with much pomp and circumstance. When he had first thought of marrying Matilda, the mere prospect of participation in such an affair had frightened him, and only as his feeling grew stronger could he contemplate it with equanimity. The event, too, would call for a foreign tour of some months, and he had not seen his way clear to relax, for even a brief period, the close attention he had always paid to the details of his large and increasing business. He had thought of late, however, that he might spare the time within a year. Certain schemes of his, long contemplated and just in shape to be taken up and pushed forward, would require some time for development, but their outcome was reasonably certain, and Matilda would not be averse, he felt sure, to an engagement of several months' duration. He had realized further that time was passing, and that if he did not marry while at least the memory of youth remained, the time might soon come when he would have little to offer a woman in return for her own life. He had no fears of a refusal. The flower he had seen blossom from the bud was his when he should see fit to pluck it.

As Truscott sat thinking thus, and waiting for Johnnie to return with the envelopes, he became conscious of the fact that the young woman to whom he had dictated his letters was sitting exactly in his line of vision, and so placed as to bring her profile sharply into view. He was vaguely aware of something familiar in the outline. Where he had seen the face, or one like it, he could not recall; but the effort to do so fixed his attention more closely upon the girl. He noted that her neck was firm and shapely, none too long and none too short, and set upon a bust revealing the graceful curves of young womanhood; and that her hair was very abundant, and of a golden-brown tint that he had always admired. As she occasionally turned a little toward him to glance at the notes before her, he caught a glimpse of her front face, which in no wise fell short of what the profile had promised. How gracefully she held her hands, and with what ease her white, shapely fingers wandered over the keys of the typewriter! Gradually, and almost before he became aware of it, he realized that the young woman who sat in the next room dutifully writing his letters, was a rarely beautiful girl. Every clerk in the office had observed the fact long before.

Truscott had never cared for young girls. Most of them he had regarded as thoughtless, silly creatures; and after passing thirty he had never thought of them except as children, and Truscott had long ago put away childish things. It occurred to him, as he sat there, that perhaps a woman might be young in years, and yet not immature in mind, and that youth might possess a charm that maturity would lack. He had noted the neatness and accuracy with which Miss Smith had written his letters; and while her choice of answers to the advertisements had not been just what he would have made, he could see that she had leaned toward mercy and given weight to considerations which a wider experience would have ignored. It would be interesting to read the letters she was writing from his notations.

When Johnnie returned with the stationery, Truscott took an envelope and addressed it to

"Miss Matilda Wedderburn,
    "1116 Oakwood Avenue,
    "City."

He blotted the address deliberately, and then picking up the letter, read it over carefully. Ere enclosing it his eyes again sought the young woman in the next room. Having folded the letter, he held it for a moment irresolutely, then tore it deliberately into strips, and these transversely into smaller bits which he held in his hand until he dropped them all together into the waste-basket.

He went out, and returning an hour later, found on his desk the letters Stella had written. These he had read over, being conscious the while that she was watching him anxiously from the next room. Having signed them without changing a word, he summoned Johnnie and instructed him to copy the letters and hand them to Miss Smith to be addressed. This done, he drew a sheet of notepaper before him and wrote;—

"My dear Matilda:

"I am glad to accept your invitation, and shall be on hand tomorrow evening, when I hope to find you in your usual health and spirits.

"Sincerely, yours,

"Wendell Truscott."

X.

Stella's work for the afternoon was light. Mr. Truscott did not come in until late, and in the meantime Stella wrote a letter to her mother, stating where she was working and why. Later on, Mr. Ross brought her a statement to copy. It was short, but the work of tabulating was unfamiliar and difficult, and the task consumed a couple of hours. Ross hovered around her a good deal during the operation and made suggestions now and then about the arrangement of the figures and the spacing of the lines. He strolled into Mr. Truscott's office and read over the letters lying upon his desk. Stella had not seen Mr. Truscott consult the bookkeeper with reference to any letters, and, while she did not know to what extent he was in his employer's confidence, Ross seemed to her to be prying into matters which were none of his concern. There was something reptilian and sneaky in his manner, that made his proximity distasteful.

She would perhaps have found it difficult to state why, but she breathed freer when he left her presence and returned to his desk in the main office. He was soon back again.

"You're doing splendid work, Miss Smith," he said, "and I wish you were going to stay with us."

Stella inwardly resolved that if she were expected to work for him, or converse with him, she would make her stay as brief as possible. When she had completed the statement and was for a moment unoccupied, Johnnie came into the room.

"Has he answered any of the letters from them plug typewriters that answered the advertisement?"

"No, Johnnie, he has not. But I don't see why you should speak of them so unkindly. There may be very good stenographers among them."

"They may be," said Johnnie, "but their looks did n't show it when they were hangin' round here yesterday. Why, Mr. Truscott would n't have one of 'em for janitor, or scrub woman! I could do better than them myself."

Johnnie had already confided to Stella several of his ambitions, the chief of which was to become a stenographer. He had a dog-eared instruction book which shared his hours of leisure with various volumes of the Young Sport's Library. And he had shown Stella, with some pride, a copy-book filled with laboriously made pothooks, the result of his phonographic studies.

"My sister's a stenographer," said Johnnie, "and she helps me. She works down at a bag factory. She ain't very far along yet, and only gets three dollars a week. But Mr. Ross has promised to help her get a better place. We might have got her in here, if she'd been advanced enough. But gee! it'll be five years before she could do it as well as you."

"How old is your sister, Johnnie?"

"She sixteen, and she a swell lookin' girl, too, she is; one of these here blonde girls with blue eyes. I've got her picture in my drawer—I'll show it to you." He went into his own room and brought back the picture.

"It's only a tintype, but she's a peach, now, ain't she, Miss Smith?"

Stella glanced at the tintype. It was a rather effective picture for its sort, of a pretty girl of a common type. Stella instinctively compared her with the showy girl who had attracted her attention the day before, though Johnnie's sister was much younger and had a much more modest expression.

"She's a pretty girl, Johnnie, and I hope she'll get a better place."

"Mr. Ross says he'll find her somethin' after a while. In the meantime, she earns a little extra by workin' for him evenings, on private business of his own that ain't got nothin' to do with the office. I use' to did n't like Mr. Ross, but since he's been so good to Nellie I think better of him. He got me a raise, too, a few weeks ago."

"It's good of him to help you, Johnnie," said Stella, "and if I can assist you in your studies during the few hours I'm here, I shall be glad to do so."

"Thank you, Miss Smith," said Johnnie. "I hope you'll stay. Old Peters wouldn't help me a bit. I'm glad he was fired. But you're a lady, Miss Smith, and I hope you'll stay."

"I'm going tomorrow, Johnnie," she replied. "I only came here to oblige a friend. Besides, I haven't been asked to stay."

"Well, I'm sure *he*'ll ask you," said Johnnie, "and I hope you'll change your mind."

The entrance of Mr. Truscott cut short this colloquy. He called Stella into his office and dictated several letters. When she carried them in for signature, he requested her to wait a moment, and she remained standing by his desk until he had glanced over the letters.

"I like your work, Miss Smith," he said, "and should be glad to have you stay with us. Have you a permanent situation where you are now?"

"No," she replied, "I'm only substituting for a few days, to accommodate Mrs. Paxton, from whose office I was sent. I'm only an amateur, and not a professional stenographer, and after the summer is over my time will be otherwise occupied."

"I'm sorry," he said, with a note of regret in his voice. "I should have liked to have you stay. I've tried many stenographers, and it's a relief to find one who knows something, and whose work does not have to be done twice."

Stella withdrew to her own room. A few minutes later Mr. Truscott came in and stood by her desk.

"Is it a question of salary?" he asked.

"Not at all," returned Stella. "I am not self-supporting, at any rate not as yet."

"You can come tomorrow, or for a few days at least?"

"I can come tomorrow," said Stella.

"Very well," said Mr. Truscott. "If you should change your mind my offer remains open until you leave—or until the place is filled."

"Thank you," said Stella.

The prospect of working constantly for and in the presence of the man who had ruined her father and robbed her mother had no attraction for her. Up to this time, the best thing she had seen about Wendell Truscott was his wish to retain her services. But that was evidently a purely impersonal matter and a part of his general business excellence. She firmly made up her mind to leave the following day. Mr. Truscott could easily find a good stenographer among those who had answered his advertisement.

XI.

Stella was slightly surprised about ten o'clock the next morning, to hear her mother's voice through the telephone. Mrs. Paxton rung Stella up from her office and then gave her place at the 'phone to Mrs. Merwin.

"I'll see you at noon, Stella," said her mother. "I wish to talk to you. I'll meet you at the Women's Exchange at twelve o'clock sharp."

Stella had many letters to answer this morning. Mr. Truscott had relapsed into his former humor, and did not even say "Good morning" when she entered his room. He dictated a good many letters, more rapidly than upon the last occasion; in fact, he kept perilously near the limit of Stella's speed. If he had gone much faster she would more than once have been compelled to ask him to repeat his words. His letters, which she had thought smoother in tone the day before, had resumed their harshness of the first day, and from those addressed to subordinates she could see that he was a hard taskmaster who mercilessly demanded his pound of flesh wherever it was due.

This trait of Truscott's character was emphasized by an incident, trifling in itself, but valuable to Stella as confirming her impressions. A beggar wandered into the office. Johnnie had gone away on an errand, and the visitor therefore escaped his lynx-eyed vigilance, and penetrated as far as Truscott's room. A whining, cringing, greasy mendicant, with one hand in a sling, a week's growth of stubble on his face, bad teeth and blear eyes, he seemed to Stella a living embodiment of misery. She heard him, from her room, begin upon a harrowing tale of misfortune, when the buzzer sounded furiously. There was no response, Johnnie being absent. A second and third time the call sounded, with increasing vigor at each recurrence, the mendicant meanwhile pouring forth his tale of woe. Mr. Ross answered the last call, making his appearance with some signs of haste.

"Mr. Ross, put this man out, and notify the agent of the building that there is a beggar on this floor. It's an intolerable nuisance, and must not be permitted."

The beggar slunk out, unaware of the sympathy that his case had excited in one heart, and of the indignation aroused in the same quarter by his summary ejectment. Stella slipped out into the hall and caught the man waiting by the elevator. She thrust a coin into his hand and experienced a thrill of virtuous pleasure when he responded in hoarse accents—

"Thank y', miss. Gawd bless yer!"

Truscott said nothing further to Stella, during the morning, about her remaining. She was somewhat surprised that he had not answered the letters of application still cumbering his desk. It seemed a refinement of cruelty to leave these poor people in suspense. Such a consideration, however, she reflected, would hardly move her employer.

Stella met her mother at the Women's Exchange at five minutes past twelve. They found a small table in a secluded corner, where they could sit alone. The waitress took their order and went to get it filled.

"Oh, Stella!" exclaimed her mother, plunging at once into the subject uppermost in her mind, "is it possible that you are working in Wendell Truscott's office?"

"Yes, mama, it is more than possible. It is an accomplished fact."

"And how does he treat you? Has he manifested any uneasy consciousness?"

"He treats me like a block of wood. For most of the time he is utterly unconscious of my existence. My immediate prede-cessor was a man who drank, and Mr. Truscott apparently did not discover for a day or two that he was gone."

"Why, Stella! I should n't think he would ignore you, for with all his villainy, he has always been hypocritical enough to profess the kindliest feeling for us. If I had not known the fundamental baseness of the man, I will admit that I should never have guessed it from his manner."

"Perhaps I've seen him in his true character," replied Stella "because I have taken him unawares and he has no motive for concealment or dissembling. He does n't know me as my father's daughter."

"Why, Stella! He could n't hear your name without recognizing you. It is only fifteen years since he held you on his knees, and fed you with bonbons."

"I wonder they did not choke me," rejoined her daughter drily. "If he knew me as Stella Merwin, the daughter of his former master and victim, perhaps it might disturb even his sang-froid. But as 'Miss Smith, the typewriter,' I was so far beneath his exalted sphere that for two days he did not even look at me, and what I might think of him is of no more consequence than the opinion of his office-boy."

"I don't understand, Stella! What do you mean?"

Stella explained the occasion of her going to Truscott's office. Mrs. Merwin had heard Mrs. Paxton's version, but not caring to manifest any special interest by minute inquiries, had restrained her curiosity until she could have an interview with her daughter. She questioned Stella as to Truscott's appearance, his manners, and his business affairs.

"I have learned very little about his business, mama, except that he employs a great many clerks, and a large force at the refinery, and that he has agents and oil-wells and pipe lines."

"Just as your father had, only the business has grown with the growth of the country. Your father would have been a very wealthy man by this time, Stella, but for Wendell Truscott."

"Suppose he asks me to stay, mama?"

"Stay, by all means! I believe he will ask you, Stella! I see more in this than a mere coincidence. It is the finger of God, pointing the way to discover the truth with regard to Wendell Truscott's perfidy and compel him to make restitution!"

Stella broke the bread into her bowl of milk, "He has already asked me to stay," she replied.

"Oh, Stella, what I hoped for has come to pass! You cannot hesitate for one moment. It is the opportunity of a lifetime! a direct interposition of Providence! I have always felt that you were destined to be the real head of the family. Your brother, George, I fear, is not of much account. He seems to be making money; he dresses well, and has his employer's confidence. But he is too frivolous for any serious undertaking, at least while he is young."

George Merwin, Stella's brother, was Mrs. Merwin's only other child. Stella's senior by several years, he had been working in Groveland for two years as clerk, and one year as assistant cashier, for a great lumber firm. He was a well-meaning youth, with a keen zest for pleasure, and a rather weak will, that made him unduly susceptible to the influence of others.

"I don't see what I can do, mama, even if I saw fit to give up my senior year at college in order to stay there."

"Stella, *you can find those papers!* It is the only way to vindicate your father's honor and punish Wendell Truscott!"

"How could I find them? I would have no access to his papers."

"They are in that safe in his office"—Stella had mentioned the safe with her father's name upon it. "Wendell Truscott was always a man of methodical habits. Mr. Merwin used to speak of the care Wendell took of papers and letters, and how closely he looked after every detail of the business. If your dear father had been more careful, and less confiding, he might now occupy the place that Wendell Truscott has usurped."

"I haven't access to his safe, mama."

"You are not yet permanently installed in his office. But once there, the scope of your duties will be enlarged. You are clever, Stella, and you're the kind of a girl men take to—you can gain his confidence in a very short time."

"But mama, it seems like treachery."

"We must fight fire with fire, Stella! Wendell Truscott stole your father's position in the business world, like a thief in the night. If there was ever an instance where the end justified the means, this case admits of anything short of crime to unmask him!"

"I don't like it, mama. I wish it could be done otherwise."

"It is your sacred duty, Stella; you would be false to your dead father's memory if you did not do all you could to establish his good name! He lives, if he lives at all, in the memory of those who knew him, as a broken man, without spirit enough to bear the burden of his misfortunes, but vainly seeking to escape them at the expense of others. It is for you, who love his memory and know the truth, to reveal to the world that

Henry Merwin was the victim, not of his own weakness but of Wendell Truscott's perfidy. You're a good bookkeeper, and he'll ask you to work on his books. You will have access to his private papers. Under any other circumstances or if you were not Henry Merwin's daughter, what I advise would of course be inexcusable. But our cause is a righteous one, and the enemy must be fought with his own weapons."

Stella's heart swelled with filial love and her blue eyes over-flowed with tears at her mother's reference to the saddest page of the family history. She answered with decision.

"Very well, mama, I'll stay. No one shall ever say that I neglected my duty to my dead father."

"You will not falter, Stella?" continued her mother impressively. "You will let no scruples stand in the way?"

"After I have once put my hand to the plough, mama, I shall not turn back. I'll tell him this afternoon that if he wishes me to stay, I'll remain for the time being."

"You're a good girl, Stella, and you make your mother's heart glad. I know you'll succeed, and already I see Wendell Truscott disgorging his ill-gotten wealth and hiding his wicked head in shame. 'Tis a long lane that knows no turning.'"

When they had finished their lunch, Stella returned to the office and Mrs. Merwin went to the hotel where she stopped on her frequent visits to Groveland. Her friends in the city were few. Henry Merwin had been up in the world when he brought his young wife to Groveland from a country village, and her acquaintances had been among the more fashionable people. She had not wished to meet them on other than an equal footing, so when the evil days came and some of them turned their faces away, she had shut out from her life a goodly number of others who would have proved her friends in adversity. She did not know this—in fact they had had no opportunity to express it—but her pride was sensitive, and thus to avoid one possible slight, she threw away the friendship of a dozen generous hearts.

"When are you going back, mama?" asked Stella, as they were preparing to separate.

"I shall go up this afternoon, by the five o'clock train. I might take the two-thirty, but I've some shopping to attend to, and I shall want to know what arrangement you've made with Mr. Truscott. What time do they close on Saturday?"

"At four o'clock," answered Stella. "I asked the office-boy this morning. If you'll wait for me at Mrs. Paxton's, I'll go home with you over night. If I'm engaged to stay, I shall have to bring down some more clothes."

"And you'll have to find a boarding place too."

"Yes," said Stella. "Mrs. Paxton is very kind, and might perhaps let me stay with her. But I wouldn't ask her to take the responsibility of looking after my meals. She is sometimes too busy to provide her own."

"No, Stella, it would be better not. I've always coddled you so at home that I fear you won't be able to get along without me. If necessary, I suppose I could come down here to stay, although I once vowed that I would never live in Groveland again until I could enjoy my own and hold up my head in the sphere where my husband placed me, which is mine, and yours, Stella, by every law, both human and divine, if the truth were but known."

"The truth shall be known, mama, if I can find it out; and you shall resume your true position in society. The longer I think of it the more strongly I feel, with you, that I am but an instrument in the hands of justice."

Mr. Truscott kept Stella fairly busy during the afternoon. When she brought in the letters he had dictated, she stood a moment by his desk until he looked up inquiringly.

"Is there anything?" he asked.

"I think, sir," said Stella, with a touch of embarrassment, "if you have n't changed your mind, that I might remain a while—a month or two, perhaps longer."

"Very well," he replied, with what seemed to Stella a strained attempt at cordiality. "I shall be glad to have you stay. I'll put you on the payroll at Mr. Peters' salary. There'll be some chance of promotion, and a sure tenure; for no one ever leaves my service, except voluntarily, if he or she observes the rules of the office and does satisfactory work."

"I'll do my best," returned Stella, sincerely enough. Whatever her ultimate design might be, she would not slight her work.

"I think there'll be no question about that, Miss Smith, nor about the result." In a good man, his tone would have seemed almost kind.

At four o'clock Stella put on her hat.

"Is it good-bye, Miss Smith?" asked Johnnie, regretfully, as she passed through the vestibule.

"Until Monday, Johnnie. I'm going to stay."

"Gee! but that's dandy! I'm awfully glad you ain't goin'. I'll have somebody I can talk to, and who'll help me in my shorthand."

Johnnie was waiting for the departure of a certain clerk.

"You can bring them cigarettes tomorrow," he said, as his victim left the counting room, "she's goin' to stay."

XII.

Stella met her mother at Mrs. Paxton's. Both ladies were delighted at her new engagement.

"I'm so glad, my dear," exclaimed her bustling friend, "that you have decided upon a business career!"

"It's only an experiment, Mrs. Paxton, a slight extension of the time I've put in for you. If I don't like it, I shall not stay long."

"You'll like it, Stella, for you have fine business aptitudes. And you'll get accustomed to the money. There's something sweet about the money one earns! Perhaps it wasn't the worst thing for Adam and Eve that they had to earn their bread by the sweat of their brow, for a reasonable amount of labor is a *sauce piquante* that nothing can replace."

When Stella and Mrs. Merwin had thanked Mrs. Paxton for her kindness to Stella, and Mrs. Paxton had settled with Stella for the three days' work, which had been charged against the refining company on Mrs. Paxton's books, the mother and daughter set out for the railroad station.

"We've half an hour, Stella. Suppose we walk out the avenue and take the train at the Ellison Street station? I'd rather like to take a look at our old home, for I feel a presentiment that we shall soon return to something like it. It was pleasant, Stella, to walk on velvet and dine off silver, and not to be obliged to look at both sides of a nickel before spending it."

The lower end of the broad avenue was lined with well-filled show-windows. Mrs. Merwin stopped momentarily to look at some striking display or other. A beautiful silk dress pattern struck her fancy.

"I should like a gown of that, Stella. My best silk is very much worn."

In a jeweler's window a magnificent diamond brooch, displayed upon a velvet cushion, sparkled with prismatic brilliancy.

"Oh, how lovely!" exclaimed Mrs. Merwin, with a sigh of admiration. "Don't you think, Stella, that that would set off a matronly figure perfectly?"

"It would become you immensely, mama; but if we don't hurry we shall miss the train."

Leaving the mercantile part of the avenue, up which the tall business blocks had gradually extended as the city grew eastward, they soon found themselves in a respectable limbo of old-fashioned dwellings, the citadels of fashion twenty years before, not given over to social clubs and select boarding-houses. These in turn were followed by more modern dwellings. Mrs. Merwin paused before one of these, a stately stone structure standing back ten or fifteen rods from the street and separated from it by an iron fence. A wide expense of velvety green lawn sloped gently upward to the house, which stood at the summit of a slight rise. Plots of brilliant-colored flowers here and there glowed like jewels in their vivid green setting. Across one half of the wide verandah a shade of gay-colored Chinese matting hung half-way to the balustrade. Near the street a half-dozen elms, large enough to have been of the aboriginal forest joined their shade to that of the grand trees lining the famous avenue, said by Bayard Taylor forty years ago to be the most beautiful street in the world—an opinion faithfully cherished by the inhabitants ever since. A gravelled path led by a graceful sweep to the front of the house and through a *porte cochère* at the side, to a vine-clad stable of pleasing design.

"This is *our* place, Stella—*was* our place—*should be* ours now—*shall be* ours, if your efforts do not fail! That was my room, the east room on the second floor. It was a dream! The pictures on the wall alone were worth more than all we now possess. The barn cost more than the house we live in. I kept my *coupé*, my carriage, my phaeton and my dog-cart. I had a coachman and a groom, and my equipage was the most admired of any in the city."

"It must have been lovely," returned Stella.

"Beyond comparison, child. And then the sense of security, of permanence! I think the greatest shock I felt, when the crash came was not regret for what I had lost, but surprise at losing it. It seemed as though the bottom had dropped out of everything! It was like a dream—where one will be sailing, sailing along—on the solid earth, too, or just above it—when suddenly, without warning, the ground fails beneath one's feet, and one wakes up, trembling, as though poised on the brink of a fathomless abyss!"

They were moving slowly as she spoke. While they were yet before the house, a carriage, driven by a coachman in livery, swept down the drive and out into the avenue. A lady, beautifully dressed, and an ugly bull dog, which sat on the seat beside her, were its sole occupants. She glanced at the two modestly attired women, turning her head toward them in order to prolong her inspection as the carriage moved swiftly away.

"She does n't know me, now," exclaimed Mrs. Merwin bitterly, "and yet *I* first introduced her into society. Her father was a German brewer, who could not speak even his own language correctly. She went to school abroad, and when she returned I took her up, and introduced her to the man she afterwards married. Her father died and left her his money, and now she occupies *my* house, and stares at me as though I belonged to some inferior order of creation! She need not hold her head so high; the hovel where she passed her infancy is still standing!"

"Perhaps she didn't recognize you, mama."

"*My* memory is not so short. I would know her forty rods away. I shall not forget this slight, Stella, when we come into our own."

"We had better hurry, mama, or we shall miss the train."

"Just a moment, Stella! I have n't looked at that house for five years, for I can't control my feelings when I see it. I always avoid it by going the other way."

They quickened their footsteps. Now and then a carriage whirled past. The air seemed all a-ring with the tinkling bells of scurrying bicyclists. Mrs. Merwin's temper, excited by this review of her past glories and the prospect of their renewal, found vent in remarks on the people whose houses they passed.

"This," she said, indicating a stately residence, "is Mr. Jewitt's place. He robs the poor with one hand and drops a nickel in the contribution box with the other. He 'holds up' the commerce of a nation, and out of the millions stolen from the teacups of the poor endows a seminary to teach his own narrow creed and glorify his name. He is worse than Wendell Truscott!"

"That couldn't be possible, Mama!" returned Stella. "But perhaps you misjudge Mr. Jewitt. Mrs. Paxton says he is very charitable, and spends millions of which the world knows nothing."

"It may be, Stella. He can spare them well enough. But whether he does or not, *he* is rich and *we* are poor, and no man could make such a fortune honestly—unless, perhaps, your father might, if he had lived long enough and had not been betrayed. We should have been enormously rich, had his plans succeeded."

They passed a palace in brown stone, with mullioned windows and a wealth of artistic ornamentation.

"The owner of that house made his money in coal. He ground his miner's wages down to the lowest notch. When he saw signs of an impending revolt, he manipulated a corner in anthracite, and, when the men struck for the bare means of keeping soul and body together, unloaded his coal on the market at high prices, and moved on Oakwood Avenue. He married his cook, who wears diamonds and rides in a carriage, while *we* walk, Stella, on the bare ground!

"This man," she said, with a sweep of her hand toward a marble pile that would have been no disgrace to Rome itself, "sold fifty tons of old iron pipe to a struggling corporation forty years ago, and took its stock in payment. The corporation had a franchise. He has not turned his hand over since, except to cut off coupons and endorse checks, and he is now supposed to be worth five millions. Your father was not like these men, Stella. *He* was a gentleman, who walked uprightly and wronged no man. From this time forth the main thing I shall live for is to see his despoiler punished—and by your hand, Stella! by your hand."

"By my hand," echoed Stella with swelling heart.

On their left, a little farther along, a stately mansion of grey sandstone stood partly concealed by a profusion of shrubbery. There was an air of chastened refinement about the place. The lawn was green, but not too green; the flowers were bright but not garish, and the profuse shrubbery lent an air of reserve to the premises quite at contrast with the gorgeous parade of opulence by which some of the residences on the street had challenged attention.

"What a lovely house!" cried Stella.

"It belongs to the only woman in Groveland whose friendship I regret and shall see again when I am restored to my own. It was not stolen by fraud or captured by the strong hand. Matilda Wedderburn inherited it from her father, who made his money honestly."

"What kind of a woman is she, mama?"

"She was my dearest friend. *She* would know me and be glad to see me, though it is five years since we met, and then only casually."

"She was at the play the other night with Mr. Truscott. He seemed quite attentive."

"They've kept company for a long time, and are supposed to be engaged. She does n't know him as he is, Stella. You must unmask him in time to save her. She is worthy of a better fate."

While Mrs. Merwin was speaking, a dog-cart, driven by a lady, approached from the direction in which they were going. The occupant of the vehicle,—Miss Wedderburn herself,—sat erect, and held the reins firmly in her gloved hands. She was driving near the curb-stone. Stella noticed that her face was radiant, as though with some sweet memory or some pleasant anticipation. As Miss Wedderburn drew near, she glanced casually at the two women on the sidewalk, gave a slight start, and made as if to check her horse. She did not stop, however, but drove on.

Stella looked around at her mother, who had turned her face away and quickened her steps perceptibly.

"Is she out of sight?" asked Mrs. Merwin.

"Yes," answered Stella. "I thought she was going to stop."

"I was dreadfully afraid she might recognize me," returned her mother, with a sigh of relief "I would have given anything to kiss her and shake hands with her. But if I had spoken to her, I should have had to introduce you. And if for any reason she should go to Mr. Truscott's office and see you there, or meet you elsewhere as 'Miss Smith,' our secret would be disclosed and our plan exposed to failure."

XIII.

Miss Wedderburn had been walking on air all day. Part of the morning had been devoted to preparations for the evening. To any one else her house would have seemed perfect already; but Miss Wedderburn moved a vase here or a statuette there, set a chair in this place or an easel in that, and arranged cut flowers in the most effective places. Her cook was ordered to prepare Wendell's favorite dishes. And, the butler was directed to bring up one of the last six bottles of a famous old wine, of which her father had once possessed quite a store.

"There's nothing too good for him," she said to herself. "This genial wine will warm his heart, my smiles will disclose an answering warmth, and he will ask me to be his."

She seated herself in the drawing-room, toward noon, to rest a few minutes before luncheon. Her little dog Dandy fawned on her and licked her hand.

"Ah, Dandy, Dandy!" she said, caressing him, "you shall have a master, and your master shall be a man, a strong man, who will love me more than you do, Dandy!"

The dog sprang on her lap and reached for her lips. She pushed him away with a merry laugh.

"No, Dandy, no, I shall kiss you no more! My lips are meat for your master, Dandy!"

Springing lightly to her feet, she ran to the piano, and soon the room was filled with a flood of melody, in which birds sang, bees hummed, waters rippled,—all nature laughed and exulted in the warmth and beauty of glorious life! The dog sat at her feet and listened solemnly.

Her brilliant runs slowed and softened, and with melting voice she sang a tender love-song. As she finished the cadence at the end of the last line, Dandy raised his voice in a discordant howl.

"Oh, you naughty doggie! How wicked of you! You should rejoice with me, and not howl so dismally! But perhaps you were just trying to accompany me, darling!" she said, taking his muzzle in her hand and shaking it playfully.

The butler appeared in the doorway. "Luncheon is served, mum," he announced, with the decorum befitting his office.

"It's a myst'ry to me," he said to himself, as he preceded his mistress to the dining-room and stood at the door as she entered, "what ladies finds to admire in them ugly pug dogs. A good bulldog or a setter or a p'inter might be of some use. Even a rat-terrier can ketch rats, but them things is jest a nuisance."

In the afternoon Miss Wedderburn visited her kindergarten. She patted the children on the head and spoke kindly to them all. They had never seemed so sweet, and her heart yearned over them. One little curly-haired maiden, in white frock and blue sash, she caught up and clasped to her heart and kissed passionately.

"You little darling," she exclaimed, "I wish you were mine!"
And then she set the child on the floor and went away.

"Miss Wedderburn's in a happy mood to-day," said the
teacher to her assistant. "She's so fond of children, I wonder
she doesn't marry and have some of her own."

Something of the same thought ran through Matilda
Wedderburn's mind as her swift horses whirled her to a meeting of the Monthly Club, where she played and sang with
unusual brilliancy. Thence she went out the avenue to her
own home, and, as she fondly hoped, to love and happiness.

Truscott kept bachelor's hall in one of the old-fashioned
houses at the lower end of the avenue. His horses and carriage
were taken care of at a neighboring livery stable. A skilful cook
supplied his table, and his man George, a negro of deepest dye,
who had been with him for many years as valet, major-domo
and confidential man generally, looked after his immediate
personal wants and officiated as butler when he dined.

It was a warm evening, and Truscott thought he would
walk up the avenue to Miss Wedderburn's. As he put on the
carefully brushed silk hat George handed to him, the glass in
the hall reflected the image of a tall, broad-shouldered man,
with a face not handsome, but masterful—that of a man who
knew what he wanted and would proceed, by the most direct
means, to get it. One would not ordinarily think of finesse
behind such a face, but would imagine his mind to be rather
the broadsword of Richard Coeur-de-Lion than the sçimitar
of Saladin, that of a man who would be more likely to break

down opposition than to avoid it, and who, having once formed a purpose, would pursue it unswervingly to the end.

And yet, as Truscott strolled slowly up the avenue, his purpose was by no means a fixed and definite one. He had meant to ask Matilda to marry him, and he was not the man to change his mind lightly. It was no sudden impulse either, nor was it an idea of recent growth that could easily be uprooted.

But strangely enough, as the hour approached he felt a pronounced return of his old shrinking—not from the responsibilities of matrimony, for his shoulders were broad enough to bear any responsibility; not from the publicity of a wedding, for he had been of late years too much in the public eye to mind notoriety. His affairs were in perfect order, his health was never better, and there was awaiting him at the other end of half a mile, a beautiful woman who loved him, a woman accomplished, rich, whole-hearted; who would preside at his table with distinction, who would make his house the resort of the best people, in the truest sense of the word, and who by her gracious gentleness would soften his own asperities. He realized that Matilda Wedderburn was the ideal woman for his wife.

And yet he felt an unaccountable shrinking from the final step. He tried to analyze this feeling and could attribute it to nothing but the mere persistency of habit. A change in one's manner of living was hard to make at his time of life. Sauntering up the avenue, now in the glare of the electric lights, now in the dense shadows cast by the intercepting foliage, he found himself speculating about the details of life with Matilda;

whether she would want him to live in her house, or whether he should prefer to build one of his own, and what sort of a house he should like to have; whether she would care to have George around, and whether he could get along without George if she didn't like him.

The avenue was quite animated. Carriages whirled their occupants toward the theaters, and here and there white shoulders gleamed through open carriage windows. The lights of passing bicycles, eclipsed in the opera glare of the electric lamps, dotted the darker spaces with points of yellow, red and green. Peals of laughter proceeded now and then from some party of gay young people, and occasional couples strolled slowly along, arm in arm. As he drew near a corner at which an electric light was suspended, he thought he recognized his bookkeeper, Mr. Ross, in company with a woman. Before he reached them, however, they turned the corner and were lost in the shadows.

"I thought Ross's wife was sick," he said to himself, "and I didn't know he had a daughter. I must ask him about his family sometime. I believe I'm developing an antipathy to that fellow, though he is an excellent bookkeeper."

The lights of Matilda's mansion gleamed through the shrubbery. Matilda met him at the door with outstretched hands and a radiant smile.

"Welcome, Wendell!" she exclaimed, "I'm glad to see you." She almost laughed in her light-heartedness. "You're the first to come," she said, "and I'm afraid I shall have to entertain you myself, for the most part. One of my guests was called out of town; another is ill. Uncle John and Aunt Hannah will be here. Uncle John is deaf, and Aunt Hannah might as well be dumb, for anything she says."

Truscott expanded under her gracious welcome.

"I want no better entertainment, Matilda. You say nothing but what is worth hearing, and whatever you do, you do perfectly."

"You're a flatterer, sir, a fulsome flatterer! But I'll do what I can. I'll sing to you"—

"You sing like an angel! Patti would turn green with envy to hear you."

"I'll play to you!"

"You could give points to Paderewski!"

"I'll feed you, Wendell. I've made you a salad with my own fair hands."

"I'm the luckiest of men, Matilda," he replied with a meaning look.

She might have forced the issue then and there, she thought, but anticipation was a pleasant emotion, and why not enjoy it a little longer? By-and-by when he had eaten and drunk, when she had discharged her duties as hostess, then she would give him an opportunity to speak, and she would answer him yes. And then she would love him, oh, how she would love him!

"Excuse me," she said, "I must see about the dinner."

She was gone but a few moments, during which her Uncle John, better known as General Wedderburn, a white-haired veteran of the civil war, came in and shook hands with Truscott. General Wedderburn had made a remark about the weather, and had put up a silver ear-trumpet to catch Truscott's answer, when Mrs. Watson, Matilda's maternal aunt, made her appearance, and both the gentlemen rose and bowed. She shook hands with them, and they had scarcely seated themselves when Matilda stood in the doorway.

"Dinner is served," she announced. "Aunt Hannah, take Uncle John's arm. Wendell, you may take me in to dinner."

She placed her hand upon his arm, and could scarcely refrain from leaning on it.

"'Sit though on my right hand,' she quoted daringly, when they entered the dining-room, "'and I will make thine enemies my footstool'. That is Scripture, Wendell! I am sure you don't know too much of it."

"I know *one* passage," he replied; "'t is from Lemuel's description of a virtuous woman:—

"'She opened her mouth with wisdom; and her tongue is the law of kindness.'"

"You're quite bright to-night, Wendell! I tried to teach you to sing, but you had no voice. But you have 'a very pretty wit,' and can turn a handsome compliment."

"'Tis you, Matilda. You would draw compliments from a marble statue tonight. What have you been doing to yourself?"

"I took a bath in morning dew, a draught of ambrosial nectar, a flight with Titania through fairyland, and I cannot get down to earth again! Perhaps a bit of fowl or a dish of pease will anchor me to *terra firma* once more."

The dinner was perfect. The general discussed it in a business-like way that precluded much conversation on his part, since he could not spare a hand to hold his ear-trumpet. Aunt Hannah spoke only when addressed. Matilda talked on a variety of topics, and Truscott proved a splendid listener.

The butler served the old wine from a cobwebby bottle. The general lifted it to his lips and tasted it with the eagerness of a connoisseur.

"'T is the old port," he exclaimed with animation. "There are but five small bottles left. You did quite right, Matilda, to reserve it for a select few, who could appreciate it. It is a rare wine. A bottle is a symphony, two bottles an epic poem; three bottles—no man could drink three bottles and stay on earth—he would be translated to Olympus. It is a drink fit for the gods, a wine for great occasions!"

"You shall help drink the other bottles, uncle. I'm saving them for my wedding."

"'Tis a wonderful wine! After drinking a glass of it, I can hear as well as ever! I drink to your early marriage, Matilda! I shall not last much longer, and it would add a sting to death to leave any of this port behind."

"To Matilda's early marriage!" said Truscott, as he touched the general's glass, and smiled at Matilda tenderly.

"We will leave you and uncle to smoke a cigar, Wendell. Here is a box I bought myself, to be sure that they were good. In the meantime, I'll play for you."

She went to the piano, and filled the house with music. Truscott passed the box of cigars to the general, and lit one for himself. He drew a few whiffs, and glanced at his companion. The general was looking at him with a strange expression. They both took the cigars from their mouths and gazed at them pensively.

"Shall we join the ladies?" said the general.

Truscott made a negative gesture. He did not wish to seem unappreciative of Matilda's cigars. Taking out his own cigar-case, he silently passed it to the general, who chose a cigar and lighted it. Truscott took another, and they smoked in appreciative silence. The music ebbed and flowed, while the smoke-rings rose in graceful spirals to the ceiling.

When they had finished their cigars Truscott placed the partially consumed cigar from Matilda's box in his cigar-case, and thoughtfully added a couple of others to it. The general looked on with a twinkle in his ancient eye and followed the younger man's example.

Matilda finished a brilliant *bravura* passage as they entered the drawing-room.

"And how did you like my cigars?" she asked, anxiously.

"They are very fine, Matilda. I liked them so well that I put one in my pocket to take away with me."

"I'm *so* glad you liked them," she said. "I felt sure you would. I'll send the rest down to your place tomorrow, since they please you so well."

"I'll promise you that no one else shall smoke them," said Wendell, feeling safe in making the statement.

Matilda played and sang to him. He did not know a note, but loved to hear her voice. She brought all her stores of wit, all the resources of culture derived from years of study, of travel, of reading and of social experience, to bear upon him. She let him read her heart, and when the general had fallen asleep and Aunt Hannah had gone to her room, she led him to the conservatory, to a cushioned seat beneath the branches of an orange tree. Electric lights of various colors peeped out from the foliage of palms and other tropical plants, and the heavy perfume of exotics filled the air. A fountain sparkled and bubbled at their side. It was the place where Matilda had determined that he should declare himself. This spot should ever afterwards be sacred to her;—she would erect a statue of Hymen upon it.

"I've known you a long time, have n't I, Wendell? Of course it is not so many years, for you are still a young man. But nowadays one crowds so much experience into so little time, that the years seem longer than they are."

He had quite made up his mind now, and would speak when the conversation gave him an opening.

"It would have seemed much longer, Matilda, if I had not known you."

She was not ready yet, not quite! She would prolong the sweet suspense for still a moment.

"I remember, Wendell, when I first saw you, at the Merwin's. It was my first ball after my coming-out party."

"And you were beautiful as a dream, Matilda!"

One moment more of liberty and then she would let him speak.

"And by the way," she mused, "I passed a woman on the street to-day who reminded me of Alice Merwin. I started to pull up my horse, but her head was turned away; I could not see her face, and therefore could not be sure it was she; so I did not stop."

Truscott scarcely heard what she was saying. He was looking into Matilda's face. It was pure in outline, clear of tint, refined by culture, and illuminated by love. It would be an inestimable privilege to go through the remainder of life with such a woman by his side. He would speak now.

"She was accompanied," Matilda went on, driven by an adverse fate, "by a tall, slender young woman, with abundant brown hair. If it was Alice, the young woman was about the age her daughter Stella would be now."

And then there rose between Truscott and Matilda the slim and graceful figure of a young woman, with blue eyes and golden-brown hair. When with an effort he banished it from his mind and fixed his eyes again upon Matilda, she seemed older; he found himself wondering vaguely how old she was. There could be no doubt about it—Matilda was growing stout, perceptibly stout. She would soon be an old woman. He was a year or two older than she, it was true, but women age faster than men. At his time of life, a woman fifteen or eighteen years younger than himself would make a more suitable wife than one so nearly his own age. He was good for twenty years more of vigorous manhood, and in half that time Matilda Wedderburn would be an old woman.

"Matilda," he said, taking out his watch, "I must ask you to excuse me. I've promised to meet one of our directors at the club after the theater, on an important business matter, and in your charming society I had entirely forgotten it! I've spent a delightful evening. In the meantime, I wish you good night and pleasant dreams."

She felt the ground sinking beneath her. With the mighty effort of a thoroughbred she recovered herself. The light had died out of her eyes, but with a brave smile she held out her hand to him.

"Good night, Mr. Truscott. I'm sorry the evenings are so short—and your business so pressing! I'll send the cigars tomorrow. Good night—*good* night!"

She watched his figure down the path, until it reached the street. Then she waked up her uncle and sent him to his home a few houses away, across the unfenced lawn.

"Good night, Matilda! I shall expect an invitation soon, to help drink the other five bottles."

"I'll send them over to you tomorrow, Uncle John," she replied with a hysterical laugh.

When he had gone she called a servant, gave orders to shut up the house, and ascended to her chamber, where she threw herself upon her bed and gave way to a flood of tears. She wept for her lost youth, for her vanished hopes. Her house of cards had fallen, and she knew not why. For the time being she recognized her defeat as a finality.

When at length she rose to prepare for the night, she stood before a mirror and gazed searchingly at her reflected image. A few hours before, hope had made her young, and her years had rolled away like a mist. Now despair had brought them back like a black pall that fell around her, shutting out love and happiness and hope. She saw before her a lonely, childless future, and a grave by which there would be none to weep.

"I am growing old," she said with a sob; then, with a flash of intuition, "There is some other woman, some younger woman."

XIV.

Stella found a boarding-place, after a little search. Since her brother was working in the city, she would have preferred a house where they could board together. She had seen him during the earlier part of the week and suggested such an arrangement.

"Well, Stella," replied George, with visible hesitation, "the fact is that Mrs. Johnson's is quite full, in the first place, and in the second place she doesn't take women."

"My idea was to find a boarding-house where they would take us both," said Stella.

"You can no doubt run across a place where you'll be comfortable," he rejoined, "and where I can see you often; and after a while, when it's convenient for me, we can get together. I'd rather not leave Mrs. Johnson's this month. In fact, I've paid my month's board in advance; and there are other reasons why I should n't care to change just now. In the meantime, if you need money or want anything very badly, why, call on me, Stella, and I'll help you out."

Stella thought her brother must be doing very well in his business, to be so free with his money. She knew what his salary had been a few months before, and had not been informed of any recent increase. She made no remark, however, upon the subject, and simply thanked him.

"Let me know your address," he said, as he left, "so that I can call when you are settled."

Upon consulting Mrs. Paxton with reference to a boarding-house, her friend recommended a certain home for young women, a very select institution, of a partially eleemosynary character, where board and lodging were furnished at cost, with refined home influences thrown in for love of humanity.

"I don't think I'd like it, Mrs. Paxton. I'm not a subject of charity—not even the most delicate and unobtrusive sort. The Merwin's have cherished their independence above every earthly thing. And I don't care to become too widely acquainted. Some of the boarders might find out my real name, which would be embarrassing, to say the least."

"Why, Stella Merwin!" exclaimed the little woman in astonishment, "you're surely not going to work permanently under Miss Smith's name?"

"I certainly mean to borrow the 'Smith' part of it, Mrs. Paxton, from her or some other one of that family—that is, if you'll keep my secret."

"But why, Stella? It was all well enough as a joke, or for a day or two, when your name was a matter of no particular consequence. But to go to work permanently on a salary, under an assumed name, looks like masquerading. But of course if you wish it"—

"Dear Mrs. Paxton! I wouldn't for the world do anything you disapproved of, and I shall have to explain why I prefer to use some other name than my own, at least in the beginning, while I'm at work for Mr. Truscott. When a young man, Mr. Truscott was in my father's employment, and when my father died Mr. Truscott took charge of my father's affairs, which were in some confusion. My mother and he quarrelled about the estate, and are not on good terms. Personally I would be nothing to Mr. Truscott, and he is nothing to me. Mama does not object to my entering his employment; in fact, there are reasons why she would like me to work there for a while. My name can be of no possible concern to Mr. Truscott. He wishes to buy my services, at the market price, and I'm willing to dispose of them on the same terms. I don't wish the situation to be complicated by any intrusion of matters personal, or old animosities. So if you'll keep my secret, I'll retain my business name for the present. If I only work for Mr. Truscott during the summer, he need never know any more about me than he learns during that period. If I'm any judge of character, the names or other private affairs of his clerks are matters of supreme indifference to him. I'm really surprised that he doesn't number them, like cabmen, or convicts, or street-car conductors."

"I'm afraid you're inclined to be romantic, Stella," returned Mrs. Paxton doubtfully. "You'll find," my dear, "that romance and business won't work in double harness. I can imagine all sorts of difficulties arising from your change of name; but then I myself would be romancing, and that wouldn't be business-like. Have it your own way, dear. I thought at first that you were ashamed of the work, and of course my professional pride was up in arms against any such attitude."

"Oh, no, Mrs. Paxton," said Stella "nothing was further from my thoughts. I think I shall like the work, and I shouldn't do it at all, if I considered it in any degree unladylike or lowering. I believe in the dignity of labor, and your example has taught me that women can do business as well and as successfully as men."

"Thank you, Stella! Well, I don't suppose there'll be any active concealment necessary. Your landlady may want a reference, and if so, I'll say that 'Miss Smith' is all right."

Stella finally found a place with a respectable widow, who took only a few boarders. Among these were a bookkeeper, a head trimmer in a millinery establishment, and a couple of school teachers—all women, and all young, at least by courtesy. Stella found them agreeable enough. She was not inquisitive, and did not pry into their affairs; and the preservation of her incognito alone would have been sufficient to render her somewhat reserved and uncommunicative. Her boarding-house was only a short distance from her brother's, and not a great way from the apartments where Mrs. Paxton conducted light housekeeping.

Stella's brother George called to see her in the evening of her first day in the new quarters. He remained only a little while, and seemed rather preoccupied, answering questions in a random fashion, and from time to time looking at his handsome gold watch, a recent purchase which Stella had never seen before.

"I'm awfully glad you're in town, Stella," he said. "A fellow needs some one to talk to occasionally, when he gets down in the mouth."

"And a girl needs a big brother to look after her, George. I shall expect you to take the best care of me."

"I'll look after you, Stella, until you get a fellow of your own, and then I suppose you'll shake me. I'd take you to the play to-night, but I've got some work to do at the office. I've been very busy of late, and have considerable evening work. I'm due there at eight o'clock. But we'll make a date soon. So long!"

Stella had hoped that he would take her for a walk, for the evening was beautiful, and the streets brilliantly lighted and filled with animated throngs. She concealed her disappointment, however, and bade him goodbye. She did not think her brother was looking as well as he ought. The once ruddy color of his cheek had faded too much, the result, she supposed, of confinement in the office, to which was also due, no doubt, his nervous and distrait manner.

"He needs more out-door exercise," she decided. "Perhaps I can persuade him to learn to ride a bicycle, and we can take long trips together in the parks, and on the boulevards, and visit parts of the city that we'd never see from a street-car."

Stella was soon settled in her new home, and ere long found herself quite absorbed in her work at the office. She found it easier as she became accustomed to the technical terms of the business, and the set formulas in which a great part of the correspondence of the office was couched. After a few weeks Mr. Truscott began merely to indicate in a word or two the tenor of his replies to letters, and she would word them herself. This of course economized his time as well as hers. Occasionally she received statements to copy or compare, and in this way became familiar with the manner of keeping the company's accounts and tracing the sources of its revenue, and learned something of the vast ramifications of a business conducted by a master mind from a very unpretentious headquarters. She saw many things that seemed unjust to her, though perhaps strictly in accordance with the commonly accepted standards of commercial morality. That a small dealer should be driven to the wall because he could not compete with a larger concern, seemed to her like predatory warfare. That a strictly legal advantage should be taken of some unimportant violation of a contract suggested highway robbery. At the same time, she was imaginative enough to recognize in the gradual but resistless growth of the corporation the work of a commanding intellect, which instinctively perceived and promptly grasped every opportunity, even out of apparent failure wresting ultimate success.

She was stimulated in her study of these matters by the ever present hope of learning the extent to which Truscott had profited by her father's failure. Her growing respect for Truscott's intellect did not blind her at all to the ethical side of the question. She knew enough of history and of life around her to understand that a man might conquer the world, and yet be indifferent to the simplest principles of morality, his success furthered perhaps, by this very indifference. That Wendell Truscott could accomplish so much and with such apparent ease, made it all the more likely that he had been guilty of the things of which he was suspected.

She found time to help Johnnie with his short-hand occasionally. Johnnie made fair progress, but worked spasmodically. He could give his attention to the pothooks for a half-hour at a time, but after that generally yielded to the superior attractions of half-dime literature. Stella sometimes looked at his books, and once read one of them through. She could easily see why it would attract Johnnie. The traditional Indian, the rolling prairie, transformed at times into a sea of fire; the bellowing herd of buffalo, sweeping all before them in their resistless rush; the buckskin-clad scout, with a vow of vengeance against the murderous redskin,—all these—had disappeared from the world of juvenile fiction; and in their train came a medley of detectives, card-sharpers, gold-miners, ball-players and prize-fighters. Comic negroes alternated with bellicose Irishmen; and wonderful inventors, generally of tender years, navigated the air, explored the depths of the sea, and penetrated to the bowels of the earth, in marvellous machines, built upon plans that were serenely indifferent to the limitations of time, space, gravity or human experience. It occurred to Stella that some writers of more pretentious novels could profit by the study of certain features of these cruder productions. The incidents, it is true, were for the most part wildly improbable; the language was sometimes offensively coarse, the characters grotesquely exaggerated; but the action was rapid and exciting; there was no padding; virtue always triumphed in the long run, wickedness was adequately punished, and the stories came to a cheerful ending; or, if perchance the hero was left in a position of deadly peril, any painful suspense on the reader's part was relieved by the assurance that all ended well in the next volume of the series, entitled so-and-so, for sale by all newsdealers.

Mr. Ross tried several times to draw Stella into conversation. But she did not like the man, and restricted her intercourse with him to the fewest words possible. Stella's manners were such that with perfect good breeding, and without giving any palpable cause for offense, she made Ross understand that his overtures toward a closer acquaintance were unwelcome. Perhaps she would have dissembled her dislike somewhat, from motives of policy, but she had already learned that Mr. Truscott did not personally admire his bookkeeper, but simply tolerated him because of his knowledge of the business and skill as an accountant. This was quite in line with her first impression, which nothing had happened to change—that Truscott looked upon his subordinates as so many machines, so many means to certain ends, the personal element scarcely entering into his consideration of them. From the point of view of a young and impulsive woman, he seemed a man without a heart—a mere force of nature, calmly and inexorably working out its appointed ends, and sweeping aside all obstacles with no concern for the incidental good or ill it might inflict. She could easily imagine that even in its incipient workings, this force as embodied in Wendell Truscott had swept her father away with equal indifference to the claims of gratitude, or duty, or faith, or honesty.

Stella's brother George came around one evening to take her to the theater. During one of the intermissions Stella saw Ross, in a distant part of the house, seated beside a young girl of about sixteen, in whom she recognized the original of the photograph Johnnie had shown her of his sister Nellie. She was rather gaudily dressed, and wore a hat trimmed with a profusion of the bright-colored flowers in fashion that summer.

"There's Mr. Ross," she said to her brother, "our head bookkeeper, sitting by the girl with the red waist."

"You must be mistaken, Stella; his name is Brown."

"No," she said, "I am sure it's Mr. Ross. I know the girl, too, or know of her. She's our office-boy's sister."

"Whew! Is she? She's a stunner! Which fellow do you mean, Stella, the one on her right or on her left?"

"The one on her left, with a mustache, and slightly bald."

"Oh," said George, nonchalantly, "I thought you meant the one on her right—the red-haired fellow; *that's* Brown. The other I don't know."

Stella saw him watching the couple furtively now and then during the evening, and once, when Ross turned his eyes in their direction, she discovered that her brother had turned and was looking another way. It did not occur to her that he might have done so in order to avoid recognition.

At the fall of the curtain, George suggested that they keep their seats a while, until the crowd should have thinned out. When at length they rose to go, he forgot his hat, and had to return for it while Stella waited in the lobby. By the time George came out, Ross and his companion had disappeared.

Stella spoke of Nellie at the office next day.

"Johnnie, how is your sister getting along?"

"Fine, Miss Smith! Mr. Ross keeps her busy evenings, and she earns as much as she does in the day time. She's goin' to buy me a watch for a Christmas present."

"Where does she work for him, Johnnie?"

"He's got a desk over in the Fenderson block, where he works evenings with another expert bookkeeper. They're over-haulin' the books of the big dry goods company that failed a couple of months ago, an' there's a whole lot of writin' in it. He keeps her busy most of the time."

Stella wondered what kind of parents the girl had, and whether they knew or cared that the girl was going to the theater with Ross, or whether they were aware that he was a married man. It seemed to Stella that they ought to know both things, and she found herself trying to figure out how she could bring the facts to their knowledge, without injuring Johnnie's prospects, or making her own part palpable. She could not of course speak to Ross. Johnnie was too young to grasp the situation. The girl would resent any interference. There was the medium of an anonymous letter, but Stella could not stoop to such an instrument, even in a good cause. She concluded that she would consult Mrs. Paxton about the matter. It was clearly none of Stella's affair, but she felt that there was villainy on foot, which ought to be prevented. Stella was very young, and had much to learn besides her employer's business.

XV.

One morning Stella wrote a letter for Mr. Truscott, addressed to a well-known local detective agency.

"Your report," the letter ran, "with reference to the person in whom I am interested, has been received and carefully read. Please send the man in charge of the investigation to call upon me tomorrow morning."

Stella had been trying to train herself to take a merely perfunctory interest in the confidential matters that passed through her hands. But she had a very active intelligence, and could not entirely restrain the lively curiosity of a fresh young mind, brought for the first time in contact with the world of affairs, and in her case, as Stella perceived, the world of large affairs. She had heard that detectives were employed by business men sometimes to learn the plans and methods of rival concerns, but oftener to watch the movements of employees holding positions of trust,—that they were, in fact, the spies of commercial warfare. As she wrote the letter, she found herself speculating as to the identity of the person under surveillance, and as to the morality of such proceedings. If it were Ross, for instance, they might be justifiable. She was conscious of a slight uneasiness at the thought that Mr. Truscott might send some one to look up her own antecedents, the discovery of which would of course spoil her chance of finding the papers;—the concealment of her name would give rise to suspicions that would doubtless result in her discharge, with the destruction of all her hopes.

Mr. Truscott was dictating to Stella at about ten o'clock the next morning, when Johnnie brought in a business card.

"This gentleman would like to see you, sir," he said, respectfully.

"Tell him to wait," said Mr. Truscott, and went on with his correspondence which he did not finish for half an hour.

"Please tell the boy to send that man in," he said to Stella upon dismissing her. Although as brief and businesslike as ever in his speech, Stella noted a decided difference in his tone, when addressing her, and felt a corresponding sense of triumph. He was coming gradually around to a realization of her quality. If dollars and cents had been involved, he would doubtless have detected at first sight that she was a person of superior birth and culture. That she could be useful in his business he had learned in a few hours, and acted upon this knowledge. That she was entitled to deference by reason of her sex and breeding he would learn more slowly. Stella hoped her stay in his office would be prolonged at least until he formed a just estimate of her character. When the day of reckoning came he would know what manner of people he had wronged, and if he had any sense of shame or remorse, this knowledge would make his punishment so much the more severe.

The individual who entered Mr. Truscott's room, passing through Stella's for that purpose, had a light step, a secretive manner, and a long nose, with a curve suggesting a Hebraic strain. He carried his hat in his hand, and closed the door of the private office behind him.

Stella's eye glanced through the outer office into the counting-room, and fell upon Ross. His usual self-satisfied expression had given place to an anxious look, and his eyes were glued to the door of the private office. Stella cut her eye at him from time to time. He stood at his desk a moment, then paced restlessly back and forth, his apprehension increasing visibly the longer the visitor remained closeted with his employer.

When the detective came out of the private office, the bookkeeper, who had left his desk was in fact waiting for him in the hall.

"Good morning, Mr. *Brown*," said Jacobs with a humorous leer.

Ross beckoned him back into a recess beyond the elevator.

"Look here, Jacobs," he said anxiously, "who are you after?"

"Well, now, Mr. *Brown*, that's a matter of professional confidence that I really *could n't* reveal. P'raps you can think of something your employer *might* need me for."

"There's no use beating about the bush, Jacobs. You know me and I know you. Are you after me?"

"Why, no, Mr. *Brown*, certainly not. How *could* you think so? You never do anything that you need be ashamed of. I do know a bookkeeper and cashier or two, however, who buck the tiger, and are well known on the shady side of Easy Street. It's quite likely their bosses would think it worth something to know where they spend their evenings."

"It's worth more to me that he shouldn't know," said Ross, immensely relieved.

"Of course," the detective continued, "a man in my business doesn't feel called on to volunteer information outside of the particular case in hand. We sell information, Mr. *Brown*, to the highest bidder, or withhold it on the same basis. We are not in business for our health."

"Take this," said Ross, hastily thrusting a roll of bills into Jacobs' large hand, which seemed to open and grasp the bribe automatically, "and I'll see you again before long. I'll arrange to meet you some evening, for it wouldn't do for me to recognize you here."

Much more at ease, Ross returned to his desk. Jacobs rode down in the elevator. At a convenient spot he counted the money Ross had given him.

"Fifty!" he observed. "That ain't bad for a little side line that the agency ain't on to! There's money in this business, if you only know how to work it. As for the gal in the office, I was n't called on to give her away—I suppose Truscott is after her hisself, and wants to git rid of the boy. A real clever detective can see things with half an eye! There may be something to be made out o' the gal later on. *I* ain't be'n in this business all these years for nothin'."

While indulging in these moral reflections, Mr. Jacobs made his way toward a certain unsavory quarter of the town, there to prosecute still further his trade of social scavenger. Men of his kind are necessary for the protection of society; but it too often happens that they do not touch pitch without being defiled.

XVII.

Stella's brother had not been to see her for several evenings. She felt disappointed and neglected, for she had relied upon George for occasional companionship during the disagreeable task she had undertaken for the benefit of the family. She was charitable enough to suppose he was working overtime, or had other engagements. A letter from her mother, however, containing a message for George, made it necessary for her to get speech with him. Upon calling him up by telephone by noon, she learned that he had not been at the office during the morning. A second call, several hours later, was no more successful, and left Stella somewhat alarmed.

"I'll go round to his boarding-house, when I leave the office," she thought. "He may be ill."

Stella was very much concerned about her brother, when she knocked at the door of his boarding-house shortly after five o'clock, and her concern was not lessened by the result of her inquiries.

"Mr. Merwin," she was told, "paid his board last night, took his trunk, and went away. We understood he was leaving the city."

Stella hastened homeward. Perhaps a letter for her had been delivered during the day. This turned out to be the case; there, upon the table in the entrance hall, lay an envelope addressed in her brother's flowing hand. She seized it with trembling, and ran up to her own room. It was short and seemed from its blotted appearance to have been written in haste:

"Dear Stella: You'll be surprised to learn that I've resigned my position, and, by the time you receive this, shall have left Groveland. A long letter of explanation will follow later on. I've been in trouble, mostly through my own fault, and have been helped out of it on condition that I go away and start life over again in the West. Break it to mother as gently as you can. I'll write her as soon as I have the nerve. Hoping that neither of you will worry, I remain, until you hear from me,
"Your unfortunate brother,
"George."

Stella was as much alarmed by the indefiniteness of this letter as overwhelmed by the news that her brother had been obliged to leave the city. She could scarcely drink a cup of tea at supper after which she went immediately to her room, where she wrote a long letter to her mother. Upon going to bed, she lay awake for several hours, imagining the kinds of trouble that her brother might have fallen into. That he had committed a crime was at first scarcely comprehensible. Perhaps it was some entanglement with a woman, though she knew of nothing to base such a suspicion upon. Of the two evils this might have seemed the more excusable in a young man. But when Stella recalled her brother's free expenditure of money, and furtive, restless, almost haggard expression at their last meeting, she could only fear the worst. Only an offense of the gravest character could merit such sudden and drastic treatment. The idea that her brother could be dishonest was inexpressibly shocking to Stella, entirely apart from the fear of public disgrace, which in this case had been eliminated. Stealing was such a low crime, and in a position of trust, like her brother's, so complicated with treachery and breach of confidence, that she tried vainly to banish her suspicion. She did not sleep well that night, and her dreams were not pleasant.

XVIII.

Mr. Truscott observed his stenographer very closely after the evening of his dinner at Miss Wedderburn's. Up to that time he had been unconscious of any special interest in the girl, and even afterwards his thoughts in regard to her were purely involuntary. A recent development in the oil business had opened up a vast new field of enterprise to the man or company that should first exploit it, and Truscott, with his wonderful keenness of perception, had been the first to fore-see its possibilities. The situation was not without difficul-ties. A large amount of capital would be required, and the undertaking must expect to meet, sooner or later, the oppo-sition of powerful rivals, who had long been seeking to con-trol the oil business of the world. To successfully head off this opposition, it would be necessary to place with pru-dence, secrecy and dispatch, a large amount of money. Most of this, of course must be disbursed through the hands of intermediaries, who must be selected with care and judgment. Truscott was a rare judge of men, and soon had his plans well under way. The new enterprise made large drafts upon his time, and, together with the regular business of the company, kept him fully employed. If Stella had left him at this juncture, he might have forgotten her; but she was in his presence every day, and habit insensibly strengthened the impression she had already made.

Stella soon became aware that matters of unusual importance were on foot. Indeed, her employer told her as much.

"Miss Smith," he said, one day, "I'm sure you fully appreciate the confidential nature of your position, and that everything you learn about the business is to be kept secret."

"I hope I have given you no occasion to think otherwise," she answered, suppressing a slight feeling of resentment.

"On the contrary," he replied, "you have given me so much cause to believe the reverse, that I mean to trust you with information which it is important should be kept absolutely secret. You will write many letters with regard to a new oil field. Some of them you will not understand, nor is that necessary. The vital thing is that no inkling of what is going on shall transpire beyond the immediate circle of those who are in my confidence."

"I think you can trust me," said Stella, her resentment fading away under the pleasant consciousness of this strong and masterful man's appreciation. It was a great pity, she felt, that he was not a good as well as a great man.

Truscott looked at her clear eye, her firm mouth, her composed bearing, and was conscious of a pleasure at the sight apart from what he saw to justify his confidence. She was not only entirely trustworthy, he was sure, but very fair to look upon.

"I'm positive of it," he asserted, with an unconscious softening of his tone. "And now will you please take dictation for me?"

He dictated not only one letter but many: some to agents in the new oil field, with reference to leases and options and purchases of land; others to coopers and tank men, about tanks and facilities for storage; others to manufacturers of machinery for refining the crude oil. The basis of Truscott's enterprise was a new process for treating low-grade oils, by which, at a very slightly increased expense over the cost of refining the higher grade crude oils, a product equally fine in quality resulted. Other letters were addressed to consumers of by-products, of which a vast quantity would be thrown upon the market in the event of success in the projected operations.

Stella was able, even with her recently acquired and still quite limited knowledge of business methods, to appreciate in a vague way the masterly skill with which Truscott's plans were laid. It was as though he were parceling out to various workmen the different parts of a vast and complicated machine, which parts when assembled at the place of erection would form a perfect whole. His letters revealed an intimate knowledge of character which made her apprehensive, now and then, lest he might, read her mind as well as he seemed to understand the mental processes of others,—their points of strength, or weakness and the considerations most likely to influence them.

With every day of Stella's presence in the office, her knowledge of the principles, the forms and the actual workings of business became more thorough. She possessed in larger measure than most women the analytical turn of mind, by which she was enabled to link cause with effect in such a manner to make clear many things which to other women would have been merely Greek; this quick and mostly subconscious reasoning indeed formed the basis of that intuition upon which Stella prided herself. At school she had excelled in mathematics, and her facility in figures became apparent to Truscott soon after she entered his office. One secret of his wonderful business success had been his quickness to recognize and utilize promptly the useful qualities of others. His was the brain of the business. He did not waste his energy in petty details. Nevertheless, since nothing human is perfect, Truscott's system was not invulnerable, as events were soon to demonstrate.

It was the head bookkeeper's duty to submit to Mr. Truscott each morning a statement of the preceding day's business, as reported to the main office up to five o'clock of the day before. It was Truscott's habit after answering the first mail to look over these statements, compare the footings, and ask explanations of any apparent discrepancy. He soon began to delegate a part of this work to Stella, handing her the papers with the request that she compare the footings and report anything seeming to require explanation. Only the next day after the conversation in which he had impressed upon her the importance of secrecy, he gave her such a statement, at the close of a rather brief dictation.

"Check that up, please, Miss Smith. You'll have plenty of time, for I shall be away from the office for several hours."

When Stella had written the letters and laid them on Mr. Truscott's desk, she took up the statement. Having footed up the debit and credit sides of the balance sheet, although she found the amounts to correspond, she somehow felt that there was something wrong about the figures. They were ostensibly correct; but the sixth sense which accompanies expertness in figures, in Stella's case as much a natural as an acquired faculty, was not entirely satisfied. A careful re-footing showed no discrepancy; the items seemed to balance. Stella was still unconvinced, when it occurred to her to compare the statement with those of several preceding days; they were all kept in a drawer in Mr. Truscott's desk, to which she had access. She took out those of the preceding week and set herself to work to trace out the error, if there were one, or to satisfy herself of the correctness of the statement.

She was not long in finding the discrepancy. In the statement of the previous day there was an entry of a payment of seven hundred dollars upon a certain account, which Stella remembered in a former statement of accounts collectible. For some reason, perhaps the nature of the account, the amount had stuck in her memory. So certain was she that the account was larger than the amount here credited as payment in full, that she looked up the previous statement. The amount stated to be due was seventeen hundred dollars. The last daily balance showed an unaccountable shrinkage of one thousand dollars in this item.

If Mr. Truscott had been present, Stella would have called his attention at once to the error. In all probability she would have awaited his return, before mentioning it, had not Ross entered her room while the statements lay spread before her.

"Mr. Ross," she exclaimed, on the impulse of the moment, "there's something wrong about this entry of seven hundred dollars in the last statement. Your report of day before yesterday shows a balance of seventeen hundred dollars due and unpaid upon that account."

"Let me see," said Ross, taking up the statement and scanning it with apparent surprise.

"It seems as though there might be an error there," he said, after seeming to compare the entries. "I'll look at the cash book and see what the item there is."

He returned to his desk and if Stella could have read his expression as he walked away from her she would have seen in it malevolence as well as annoyance. He soon returned.

"It is a double error," he said, with a show of frankness, "a most incomprehensible error. Such a thing never happened before in my bookkeeping. It has gone into the cash as seven hundred dollars, and of course has followed that in this statement. I would n't have had it happen for the difference between the two amounts. I'll correct the error at once, Miss Smith, and you will do me a favor by saying nothing about it. I'm sure Mr. Truscott would not like it, and we employes ought to stand together. You won't mention it, will you?"

"No," replied Stella, "if the error is corrected I don't see why I should. Mr. Truscott will never know the difference, for he handed the statement to me without looking at it. All he would do in any event would be to call your attention to it for correction, and if that is done, beforehand, I don't see why he should be troubled with it."

"You're very good, Miss Smith," said Ross, with perceptible relief. "There's nothing more annoying to a man who depends for his living upon a reputation for accuracy and skill, than to be caught napping in such a way."

He took the statement and soon returned it corrected. The figure one had been added before the entry of seven hundred dollars. The incorrect figures in the footings had been carefully erased and the correct amounts substituted. Having run over the footings again, Stella marked the statement "O.K.," laid it on Mr. Truscott's desk, and dismissed the subject from her mind. The incident, however, was not lost upon her; it brought home to her impressively the importance of accuracy and care in handling the mass of detail that made up the volume of a large and complicated business.

XIX.

A week had elapsed after George's disappearance before Stella received another letter from her brother. In the meantime she had run down to Cloverdale to apprise her mother of George's disappearance and show her his somewhat vague and incoherent note. Mrs. Merwin was greatly distressed.

"Surely, Stella," she cried, "what you suspect cannot be true! He has merely got into some boyish scrape."

"No, mama," replied Stella, "I do not believe George would leave a place where he was doing so well, except for something serious. He says he was in trouble, and the letter,"—she held it in her hand—"is sufficient evidence. George throws off care too easily to write in this strain without the gravest reasons."

"You are not a bit of comfort to me, Stella! You always look on the worst side of things. It seems like treachery to your dear father's memory to believe that his son could be capable of—of what you find so likely! I would n't have thought it of you, Stella!"

"There is a way to make certain, mama."

"To make certain that he hasn't done anything? If there's a way to do that, I should like to know it."

"To make certain whether he has or not."

"Stella, you don't understand a mother's feelings. I'd rather remain in doubt than to know that he had done wrong."

"We can ask his employers, and they will probably tell us the truth. If there *is* anything wrong there, they have surely been very considerate!"

"No, Stella! I'd rather wait until I hear from my poor boy himself. There might be things which would appear to them in one light, and that George might explain so that they would seem entirely different. There's been nothing in the papers about it, and if his employers have chosen to ignore it, why should we, of all people, stir it up? He says he has been helped by a friend. In all probability, whatever he did was known to only a few. It may have been kept from the knowledge of his employers, and any inquiry of them might rouse suspicions that would work to George's injury."

"We'll surely hear from him soon," Stella replied, "and meantime we'll let the matter rest."

"A sister can never feel a mother's love, Stella," complained Mrs. Merwin. "A mother does not so easily believe ill of her children."

Mrs. Merwin talked in this strain for some time, and then the conversation turned on Stella's undertaking.

"If *you* had made greater headway, Stella, George might not have been exposed to temptation, and surely would not have needed to rely upon strangers for help. Is there any hope of your finding the papers soon?"

Stella gave her mother some idea of the extent to which she had gained Truscott's confidence, and of her growing familiarity with the business.

"If we were vindictive, Stella," said her mother, "you might be able to do him incalculable harm, and no more than he deserves. But we do not want revenge, we simply want justice, though he ought to be exposed. What do you think of Wendell Truscott, Stella, now that you know him well?"

"I think," said Stella, "that he is a strong man, who gets what he desires. My father was a good man, and an able man. Mr. Truscott is a strong man. I could not say as yet that he is unscrupulous;—he no longer needs to be. But I think he would not hesitate, if he felt it necessary, to sweep aside anything or anybody that stood in his way. I have not learned him thoroughly yet: I don't know that I'm capable of taking his measure. So far, he overpowers me. We know that he has robbed us. I believe him to be entirely capable of it, if the end to be gained were of sufficient importance. That being so, I could not respect him. And yet—when he speaks, I feel as though I have to obey him—not simply because I am paid, but because I can't help it."

"Stella, my child, you must not let that feeling sway you! You must bear constantly in mind the sacred nature of your undertaking. Wendell was always that way. He wound your father round his fingers, and led him to ruin. Wendell Truscott is a snake in the grass, and fascinates people only to destroy them! But we'll show him, Stella, that two can play at that game. Your father did not know him;—we do. You are partly in his confidence. He has no reason to distrust you. Before long his secrets will be open to you, and then the truth shall be known!"

Stella, though her opinion remained unchanged, acquiesced in her mother's views in regard to George, and making no further inquiries, awaited patiently the promised letter of explanation. It came at the end of the week, with a Far Western postmark, and ran as follows:—

"Skull-and-Crossbones, Dak., Aug., 18.

"Dear Stella:—

"I suppose I've got to write you and mother an explanation of my erratic conduct. I said enough in the note I wrote you to suggest that I was in serious trouble, and now I'm going to make a clean breast of it. It's bad enough as it is, but, if I did n't explain, you might think it still worse. I can't write this to mother, but I know you'll make it seem the best you can, Stella.

"The fact is, that I fell into bad company, and got to gambling, and began, after a while, to frequent a gambling house. It is no trouble to find them, in spite of the police, and you'd be surprised at the men one meets at such places. I've played many a time against your chief clerk, Ross, a 'high roller,' by the way, your boss had better watch him. Of course I had n't much money to lose, and when luck went against me I commenced to borrow from the firm's funds. It was easy enough, for I had the handling of the cash. I meant only to borrow it, Stella, and to pay it back to the last cent, which I did—but I have n't got to that yet.

"Of course I knew this was dangerous, and several times I stopped for weeks at a stretch. But the fascination of it would sooner or later draw me back. I stopped for a week or two after you came to town; but I was soon at it again, and for a while I had a run of good fortune. Then my luck changed; I lost all my surplus. I could have stopped even—but I did n't. I believed in my luck, and the next day borrowed a couple of hundred dollars from the firm; I did n't have to make up my account until the end of the week, by which time I figured that I could easily repay the loan. But my luck did n't improve; before the end of the week I was a thousand dollars behind. There was only one way out of it, and that was to doctor the books. A couple of false entries made everything apparently right, and still left me time to recover myself—before the monthly balance sheet was due.

"But all this, Stella, is only the prelude to a certain night. What I borrowed from the safe that Monday night before I went away, left me fifteen hundred dollars in debt to the firm—I put it that way, Stella, for I fully intended to return it. Luck was against me at first, then in my favor, until I had two thousand dollars on the table. At that moment I could have repaid my loan and would have been five hundred dollars to the good. But the fever was in my blood. I could see nothing but the green cloth and the whirling wheel. I staked the whole amount—and lost!

"Put yourself in my place, Stella! I was ruined, disgraced, and I should drag down the family name. I had a revolver in my pocket and my hand had sought it, when some one seized my arm. The police had raided the place. I was arrested, deprived of my weapon, and taken to the police station.

"I expected of course nothing but exposure. But an unknown friend came to my rescue. A gentleman visited me at the police station early the next morning. He had heard of my misfortune, he said, and had his own reasons for being interested in my future. If I would make a clean breast of everything, he would try to help me out. I didn't know his motives—don't know them yet—can only judge of them from what he did. He might have been a police spy; but I knew that nothing I could say would make my situation any worse, and would have clutched eagerly at any straw. I told him everything. To make a long story short, he gave me the money to repay my loan, on condition that I leave Groveland immediately. He offered to find me employment, and gave me a letter to the superintendent of the ranch where I am now, which belongs to a friend of his. I am doing well, have turned over a new leaf, and will never touch a card or make another bet. I have not been able to learn my benefactor's name; but he has my undying gratitude and I hope to prove that I was worthy of his help.

"Give my love to mother, Stella, and in the meantime believe both of you that I am sincerely repentant. Thanks to my good genius, I was able to turn over my books and accounts in proper shape, before suspicion had been aroused, and the story of my misdoings is known only to you, to my anonymous friend, and to myself. I state it hereby way of confession and humiliation, and because you ought to know. Hoping that you and mother will not think too hardly of me, I remain, sincerely,

"Your repentant brother,
"George Merwin."

This letter was to Stella at once disturbing and reassuring. The letter was frank enough as to the main facts, but the pitiful parade of borrowing and lending revealed a certain self-deception, which if genuine was not the best guaranty for her brother's future. The immediate danger was, however, over, and there was nothing now to fear except the inherent weakness of character which, having once yielded to temptation, might find it hard to resist when it came again, as it inevitably would. Before going to bed she wrote a long letter to her mother. Her first thought was to state merely the substance of her brother's story, in a way to make as light as possible the blow to her mother's pride and affection. But second thoughts advised her that maternal love would furnish every needed palliative. She therefore enclosed the letter with her own.

"It is serious enough," she wrote, "but it might have been worse. He seems to have taken the lesson to heart. I send you his letter; it speaks for itself. Who the good genius was that rescued him I cannot imagine. Perhaps you may be able to review the past and find some one with sufficient interest in the family to perform such an act. If we can, we ought to find out who he is and thank him. We could not say too much."

Stella found the reply to this letter when she reached her boarding-house in the evening of the next day:

"Dear Stella:—George's letter has pained me deeply, but it ends the suspense. Of course he is somewhat to blame, but the men who led him into temptation are much the more culpable. George was always too easily influenced. I've sometimes considered you stubborn, Stella, and have often wanted to shake you because you insisted on having your own way. Alas! I wish now that poor George were more like you! I shall tremble for his future even yet, but if a mother's love and a mother's prayers can help him, they shall not be lacking.

"One thing about this transaction, Stella, that I do not understand, is, why any one should pay two thousand dollars to get George out of trouble? If it were ten dollars, or a hundred, one might conceive of some rich philanthropist helping a young man out of trouble for the love of humanity. But it's contrary to ordinary human experience for a man to spend so much money for such a purpose, *unless he had a powerful motive!* His method, too, is inexplicable upon any other hypothesis. Why, otherwise, should my boy be hurried away from the city before having time to bid his mother farewell. It looks like a deep-laid scheme, Stella. The philanthropist was evidently waiting at the jail door. There is something mysterious about the whole matter, and mystery implies evil. Honest men do not need to hide their good deeds. I don't know, among all my acquaintance, a single person to whom I could ascribe such magnanimity. Matilda Wedderburn might be capable of it; but she is a woman, and would be unlikely to know of George's troubles; and she would have no motive for concealment.

"May not this be the most reasonable explanation? Wendell Truscott, seeing your brother on the threshold of a successful business career, becomes apprehensive lest George may in future learn the truth about the origin of Wendell Truscott's wealth. Trouble by a guilty conscience, he sets his spies on my boy's track, and perceiving a favorable opportunity, takes advantage of it to remove George as far as possible from the sphere of his own activity. He might have crippled George's power for harm by letting him be disgraced and sent to prison. But such publicity would have recalled attention to your father's career and might have led to unpleasant comment concerning Truscott; for I cannot believe that the world has forgotten so great and so good a man as your father, and many would have asked why Henry Merwin's son should be poor and in disgrace, while his former clerk had grown fat on the proceeds of Henry Merwin's genius! Nay, more, Stella, from what we know of this man, who robs the widow and the orphan, and is dead to every human feeling, I am convinced that *he himself* set the trap into which poor George has fallen! *He* set others to lead George into temptation, that he might get him out of the way! The scheme was worthy of the dark and devious windings of Wendell Truscott's mind. Mark me, Stella, we shall yet see, when you accomplish your mission and Wendell Truscott is exposed, that he was at the bottom of this wickedness as well. You must make haste, Stella. We cannot tell what his next step may be. He has no high opinion of our sex, as you have discovered, but if it should occur to him that we might be dangerous, what could we do against so powerful an enemy? You cannot utilize too soon the opportunity to set your father's memory right and restore us to the place in society which should be ours by every law of God and man! And I am more firmly convinced than ever, Stella, that justice will prevail, and that soon! Something tells me that ere long the truth will be disclosed. I am not mercenary, and could be content with poverty if it were merely the result of misfortune. But I can never rest while I see another enjoying what should be my children's and my own. Lose no time, Stella, if you love me! God is with us, and you cannot fail!

> "Your loving mother,
> "Alice Merwin."

Stella lay awake a long time turning over in her mind the thoughts to which this letter gave rise. That Mr. Truscott could in any way have been involved in her brother's affairs had never occurred to her, but she now recalled a dozen circumstances consistent with such a theory. There was the letter by her employer addressed to a detective agency, and the subsequent private interview with a mysterious and crafty looking personage. She had seen Ross at the theater with Johnnie's sister, and recalled George's strange conduct on that occasion. She knew from her brother's letter that he had known Ross as "Brown," and his first recognition of Ross as Brown. It seemed quite plausible that the bookkeeper, by Truscott's order, and under the shield of an assumed name, had wormed himself into a careless lad's confidence and led him carefully into a trap. She had long since discovered that Ross was personally disagreeable to Mr. Truscott. Perhaps one reason why he was retained in the business was his usefulness as a tool for unworthy ends.

Stella sickened at the thought of such wickedness. If there had only been herself to consider, she would gladly have thrown up her task in disgust, so revolting was the fabric of dissimulation and crime with which she was brought into such intimate contact, and to which she was doubtless each day unknowingly contributing. She had involuntarily begun to respect, in a measure, the intellectual power of her employer, and to ask herself, somewhat regretfully, why he should find it necessary to stoop so low in order to acquire what he was abundantly equipped to obtain by honest means. But now she mistrusted her own judgment. She had sometimes criticised her mother's proneness to impute motives to others, sometimes upon very slender premises. But in this case her mother, who was older and wiser than she, was surely right. Stella felt that she had been unduly influenced by Truscott's strength of will. She would henceforth remember that craft, while commonly associated with weakness, was not incompatible with strength, and that the two combined might prove a well nigh irresistible force—such a force, indeed, as she had already dimly perceived Wendell Truscott to be in the industrial world. She must be on her guard, and finish her work while Truscott's mind was too fully occupied with his great enterprise to waste time in seeking out possible enemies whose sex and obscurity were likely to render them harmless.

XX.

A carriage, driven by a liveried coachman, drew up before the El Dorado Building, one fine morning in Summer. A lady alighted, and having ordered the coachman to wait, entered the building and stepped into the elevator.

"Eighth floor, please," she said to the operator.

In less than a minute, the intervening floors were passed, the lady being the only passenger. The elevator came to a stop, and she stepped out upon the mosaic floor.

Mr. Truscott had dictated his first batch of letters, and was closeted with one of the directors of the company. Stella had just begun her work of transcribing, when she heard a feminine voice, in well-bred accents, addressing Johnnie in the ante-room.

"Is Mr. Truscott in?"

"Yes'm," the boy answered in his most respectful tone. "He's engaged just now. Shall I tell 'im you're here?"

"Oh, no," she said, "I don't wish to disturb him. I'll wait until he is at liberty."

"You'll find a better seat in the next room, ma'am," said Johnnie, showing the lady into Stella's room, where he set a chair for her near the window.

Stella saw a tall, handsome woman of about thirty-five, with a stately, high-bred air, and dressed in a simple but rich gown—just such an ideal of patrician elegance as Stella had often pictured herself—aside, of course, from the question of age,—when the Merwins should have their own again. She also recognized in her the Miss Wedderburn whom she had seen with Mr. Truscott at the theater, and of whom her mother had spoken so warmly on their walk out Oakwood Avenue.

Stella, after a brief glance at the visitor, went on with her work. The lady, after sitting for a moment, rose and went to the window, where she stood looking out over the lake.

"What a beautiful view," she exclaimed, turning partly toward Stella.

"Yes," said Stella, "the lake is very beautiful, at most times."

"It is said to be fickle in its moods," replied Miss Wedderburn. "I have seen it calm and peaceful, and in an hour or two it would be lashed into angry waves."

"And every changing mood brings out some new beauty," said Stella. "What would an artist not give to paint the different zones of color, lying one beyond the other, and the dark patches where the cloud-shadows fall?"

"Yes," returned Miss Wedderburn, turning more toward Stella and giving her a searching glance, "it would be a fortune to a poet to sit by this window, as you do, and watch the varying phases of the lake—in calm, in storm, in sunshine and in rain. Its beauty, too, is all its own; it does not depend upon encircling mountains, or crumbling castles, or mouldy palaces, or other romantic associations. You enjoy quite a privilege. Have you been here long?"

"Only a few weeks," said Stella.

"Will you pardon me if I ask your name?" asked Miss Wedderburn, impulsively. "I have a reason for asking."

"Miss Smith," answered Stella, with a conscious blush. She had no scruples about assuming the name, but she had never become hardened to the direct lie. As to Truscott, the deception was justifiable, as to others, harmless; yet old inherited prejudices in favor of the literal truth made her, at times, somewhat uncomfortable.

Miss Wedderburn seemed a trifle disappointed.

"Your face and your voice remind me so much of a dear friend of mine, of whom I have seen but little for a number of years, that I hoped you might have been her daughter."

Stella, conscious of a narrow escape, began to work upon another letter, in order to shut off the conversation. Miss Wedderburn watched the girl's slender fingers fly over the white keys and her gaze strayed again to Stella's face. This young woman was no ordinary office girl. She had observed the office type, and something in this young woman's speech and manner marked her as at least a remarkable exception. Miss Wedderburn was struck, suddenly, by an unpleasant thought. Perhaps this beautiful clerk was responsible for the change in Wendell Truscott, so apparent on the evening he had dined at her house! She knew of no woman besides herself to whom he had been attentive. Only a man of unusual shortsightedness or extreme preoccupation could have failed to discover in this girl both beauty and refinement. Every word of that interview in the conservatory was written on her memory in letters of fire. She recalled, too, having seen this girl on the avenue, in company with the woman she had thought might be Alice Merwin. She had mentioned the meeting to Truscott, and had described the girl, who had been in Truscott's office at that very time! She was busied with these thoughts, which filled her with disturbing emotions, when the door opened and a gentleman came out of Mr. Truscott's private office,—a man a little past middle age, and evidently an acquaintance of Miss Wedderburn, to whom he bowed low and held out his hand.

"How do you do, Miss Wedderburn? The sight of you is good for sore eyes. I haven't seen you for—let me see?—it must have been a year!"

"It's your own fault, Mr. Dalton," returned Miss Wedderburn giving him her hand. "I live at the old homestead, at the same number, on the same street, where I lived for—well, I'll not say how long, for it would make you seem too old."

"Yes, yes, Miss Wedderburn, it's all my fault, and I must correct it! I'm coming to see you very soon. Your father was a great friend of mine and you grow more and more like him. What a wonderful thing is heredity! A homely man may have a beautiful daughter—"

"Now, Mr. Dalton, you must not slander my father under the shelter of compliments to me. I shall not permit it."

"Well, we did n't exactly admire Wedderburn for his beauty. Even your mother never claimed that he was more than good looking! He had other qualities that endeared him to his friends. But I was speaking more generally—at least so far as *he* was concerned. I was about to say that a homely man might have a beautiful daughter, their faces differing entirely in detail, and yet you see the father's face in the daughter's as clearly as if it were reflected in a mirror."

"You could n't pay me a higher compliment, Mr. Dalton. You really *must* come to see me now."

"Yes, my dear, I will, I will! How vividly the sight of you brings up the old times when your father and I and poor Henry Merwin were cronies, and dined together at the club every day, and almost lived at one another's houses! It was too bad about Henry, too bad—too bad! There was something mysterious about his failure; it never was satisfactorily explained."

Miss Wedderburn's eyes had strayed toward the girl at the typewriter, who had stopped writing and was listening intently. Her eyes were sparkling, and her cheeks alternately paled and flushed.

"If there is anything in what Mr. Dalton is saying," thought Matilda, "I would say that I see Alice Merwin looking out of this Miss Smith's eyes. I must find out more about her."

During this colloquy with Mr. Dalton, Johnnie had announced Miss Wedderburn. Truscott came forward from the inner office to meet her.

"Good morning, Matilda," he said, with outstretched hand.

"Good morning, Wendell! Can I see you a moment, on a matter of business? I want your advice. Mr. Dalton here has been flattering me, but I want you to be serious."

"Wendell is never anything but serious," chirped Mr. Dalton. "Well, good morning, my dear, I really *must* come to see you."

Miss Wedderburn had met Truscott only once since he had dined at her house, and that in the presence of others. After the keenest edge of her disappointment had worn away, her case did not seem so utterly hopeless as at the end of that fateful evening. Wendell had known her for fifteen years and had not yet asked her to marry him, yet she had never despaired. Why begin now? True, that had seemed the psychological moment; but there might be other occasions still more favorable. *She* would not change, and perhaps Wendell would, and when they should both be of the same mind, the result would be more satisfactory. She would bide her time.

Matilda's wealth was largely in personal property—stocks and bonds and such investments as would produce an income with the least amount of personal attention. The late Mr. Wedderburn had thought thus to relieve his daughter of the responsibility involved in the care of houses and lands or the management of commercial enterprises. It was necessary, however, for Miss Wedderburn to keep track of her investments, and she bought and sold occasionally as circumstances seemed to warrant. She had the best legal advice, but now and then consulted her business friends, and especially Truscott. When a financial question arose, it was only natural, he being so much in her mind already, that she should think of him in that connection.

Stella felt strangely uneasy during this consultation. She was conscious of an incipient hostility to this fine lady closeted with her employer. Miss Wedderburn, it seemed to Stella, ought to be able to meet Mr. Truscott often enough in society, without following him to the office and interrupting him, at a time when the urgency and importance of his affairs demanded the closest attention. It really seemed—unladylike! Stella cared nothing for the man, of course, but she did like to see people observe the proprieties. Miss Wedderburn was old enough to know better,—indeed, Stella thought a little spitefully, perhaps so old that she could do things that would not be proper for a younger woman.

Mr. Truscott gave Miss Wedderburn his views on the subject of certain municipal bonds. When she rose to go she put out her hand.

"Well, good-bye, Wendell! I'm ever so much obliged. Come and see me soon!"

"I will, Matilda," he answered, earnestly. "And don't hesitate to ask my opinion at any time. It may not be of much value, but such as it is, you are welcome to it."

She had said nothing to him about Miss Smith. On second thoughts it was better to seem to ignore the girl's existence. A woman who worked for her living could hardly prove, upon a fair field, a formidable rival to Matilda Wedderburn, whose social and other advantages ought easily, with a man like Wendell Truscott, to outweigh mere youth and beauty. If they were not to compete on even terms—but Miss Wedderburn blushed for the thought, it was unworthy of her and of Wendell Truscott. Nevertheless, she resolved to keep her eye on this young woman, and to learn, as occasion offered, something of her antecedents and present circumstances.

As Miss Wedderburn swept out of the office, she glanced at Stella with a cold smile, and as their eyes met, each was conscious of a distinct feeling of antagonism.

XXI.

Stella had been very busy for a week or ten days. Mr. Truscott's scheme was making rapid headway, as she knew from the tenor of his replies to the letters received at the office. The most important letters, as well as carbon copies which Stella made, were kept under lock and key in Mr. Truscott's desk, or put away in the safe by his own hand.

She found herself becoming more and more interested in the enterprise, and more deeply impressed than ever by Mr. Truscott's intellectual clearness of vision and comprehensiveness of grasp. Viewing the situation from the inside, she was able to see the whole plan of campaign and watch the course of events as could no one else but Truscott himself.

For Stella had gathered from the correspondence that not even any one director of the corporation knew all the details of Truscott's plan. Of one he distrusted the discretion—he was liable to talk; of another the intelligence—he could not appreciate the importance and delicacy of certain negotiations. Truscott never seemed to question Stella's discretion and dictated to her letters so confidential that the recipients were told to return or destroy immediately.

Stella could not at first but feel flattered, by these marks of confidence. It seemed as though her employer regarded the matter as settled, once for all, by what he had first said to her. She was conscious later on, of a slight feeling of pique that he never said anything further to show his appreciation of her trustworthiness. She would have liked to know certainly whether this silence grew out of the perfection of his confidence, or whether he had so small an opinion of her intelligence as to suppose that she could not appreciate the importance of what passed through her hands. There was a certain humiliation in the thought that this masterful, resourceful man might regard her as a mere piece of office furniture—a modern business appliance, like the telephone or the telegraph. She had noticed that men called the writing-machine and the operator "typewriters," indiscriminately; whether the custom grew out of a poverty of language or a confusion of ideas she did not know. In either event the fact was not flattering to the operator's intelligence.

Stella, who was prone to introspection, ascribed this annoyance at her employer's seeming obliviousness to what could be its only source—the desire to so impress Wendell

Truscott with her intellectual capacity that he would properly respect it when called to task for his past misconduct. She had learned to admire the force of Truscott's character, and wished him, when in the future they should meet upon a more equal footing, to think as highly of her own. Thus she accounted for the seeming incongruity of her desire to gain the good opinion of a man whom she had every reason to despise and hate. It was therefore with a thrill of exultation that she received from him one morning a decided mark of the highest confidence. She had brought in her transcript of the first batch of letters dictated, when Truscott said:—

"Miss Smith, I wish you to take more complete charge of my correspondence. I will give you the combination to my private safe, and will expect you to file with your own hands such letters as I shall indicate. I have n't the time to do it, and I can trust you."

He showed her how to open the safe, and as the thick door swung open under his manipulations of the lock, Stella viewed with heightened pulse the interior of this repository, where in all probability might be found the evidence to vindicate her father's memory, and restore her mother's rights. A certain sense of proprietorship came over her, too, at the thought that this safe was once her father's, and by right should now be hers.

"Here are the various boxes," said Truscott, pointing them out, "for different kinds of papers and letters. All documents should be carefully filed, so that they can be found in a moment; for in business, as you must have learned ere this, there are times when delays are dangerous.

" 'There is a tide in the affairs of men,
Which taken at the flood, leads on to fortune'."

Stella was surprised to hear him quote even so trite a passage. She had not supposed that he ever thought of anything but business. He might have read in her expression something of this feeling, had he been looking at her at that instant.

"Of course," he went on, "I do not mean to increase your responsibilities without corresponding compensation. We are going to reorganize the office at the end of the month, in order to take care of the increased business; and I'll see that you are properly looked after."

"Thank you, sir," replied Stella gratefully. Upon first entering the office she had merely used the conventional "yes" and "no" in speaking to him; but the habit of subordination had unconsciously so grown upon her—perhaps the example of the other clerks had not been without its effect—that she instinctively added the title of respect whenever she now addressed him.

After bringing her a few letters and papers to file under his supervision, he closed the interview by showing her how to close and lock the safe.

In the evening Stella found at her boarding house a characteristic letter from Mrs. Merwin:—

"What is the matter, Stella? Have you forgotten the great work to which you are called? I have not heard from you for three days.

Dear Stella, do not falter! I feel more certain every day that we are on the eve of success. If you will do your part, we shall soon be placed right before the world!

"I have just been thinking, Stella, of what we shall do when we recover our property. Perhaps it would be as well to go abroad for a while, rather than return to Groveland. My heart is too full of bitterness towards them for me to meet my old acquaintances with a smiling face. Perhaps a year or two of travel in Europe would modify my feelings. Then, unless you should marry some foreign nobleman, we could settle in Groveland. I should like to buy the old place, where I lived so happily with your dear father, and where you and George were born.

"I shall have my dresses made, of course, in Paris, and it will probably be cheaper to buy our diamonds and laces there. But since you may not get our affairs settled before late in the Fall, and as I could n't think of crossing the Atlantic in the winter, we may have to manage until Spring with what we can buy here.

"You must make haste, Stella, for this suspense is killing me. I had a severe attack of palpitations yesterday, and Dr. McLean advises absolute rest and freedom from worry. But how can I stop worrying, under the circumstances? My health is in your hands.

"I have not heard from George. Has he written you?

"Your loving mother,

"Alice Merwin."

This letter gave to Stella a slight sense of discomfort. Her mother, she realized, was going too fast, and building too confidently on what was only a possibility, or at most a probability. That Truscott had defrauded her father there could be of course no question, but that she would find the means to prove it was quite a different proposition. So long as her mother confined herself to mere speculations concerning their future movements no great harm would follow. But she must be prevented from injuring her health by worry, or running into debt on the strength of her great expectations. Before going to bed she answered her mother's letter thus:—

"Dear Mama:—I have received all your letters, and you must forgive me for not having answered them sooner. I have been making progress in our affair, but you must not be impatient, nor raise your hopes too high. If Mr. Truscott was as prudent in this matter as in others, he may long since have destroyed all evidences of crookedness in his dealings with papa. Be patient, and I think it quite likely I shall be able to report decisive results before very long. Take care of yourself, for of what avail would be success, if you were not able to enjoy it? I would not trouble myself, if I were you, about how the money is to be spent, until we are sure of getting it. A trip to Europe seems to me like a dream of delight, but if we do not succeed I can live very comfortably in 'my ain countree.' I will answer your letters more promptly hereafter.

"Yours lovingly,
"Stella."

XXII.

Stella stood by the window, looking out over the lake. During the night a thunderstorm had cleared the atmosphere. A landward breeze kept back from the lake the smoke that might otherwise have marred a beautiful view. The wind was just strong enough to send the water in little crested wavelets against the breakwater. The delicate blue of the sky met in a clean cut line the darker azure of the sea. Here and there, in the distance, a steamer trailed behind it a black streamer of smoke, and the graceful lines of the revenue cutter at anchor in the harbor reminded Stella of a floating swan. With a field glass which she had brought to the office, she could see the men holystoning the deck, polishing the brasses, and otherwise setting the ship in order.

"It's a beautiful sight, isn't it, Miss Smith?" said a voice behind her.

Stella started, and almost dropped the glass.

"You startled me, Mr. Ross, you came in so quietly." Ross's cat-like ways irritated Stella, and had been originally the main cause of her dislike for him, which had become a stronger feeling since she had learned of his evil influence upon her brother George. Only the weakness of her own position, and the necessity of maintaining her assumed character, had enabled her to dissemble, so far, her indignation.

"You were so absorbed, Miss Smith, that you didn't hear me. When you have watched the lake for ten years, as I have, its novelty will have worn off, and you will see in it only a fickle, treacherous monster, that swallows all that comes within its grasp."

"You have been here a long time," said Stella, constrainedly.

"Ten years," he replied. "I've watched the business grow from a struggling concern, and I hope I may see it expand to even double its present proportions."

"You will see that and more," said Stella, unconsciously partaking of his enthusiasm, "and in the near future."

"What do you think of the new reörganization plan?" he asked innocently. "Doesn't it strike you a wonderfully bold and comprehensive scheme?"

Stella recognized with a start the drift of the question, and the importance of the answer which had slipped from her lips in an unguarded moment. The realization of her indiscretion put her upon the defensive.

"Just look," she exclaimed with enthusiasm, "at that little yacht outside of the breakwater, how gracefully it rides! Its sails are like wings—it skims the water like a bird. Are you fond of sailing, Mr. Ross?"

"Yes," he said. "I like Summer excursions—when I have agreeable company," he added with a smile that was half a leer.

"Oh, I love the water," continued Stella, "I could live on it! If I were a man I should be a sailor."

A clerk summoned Ross to the counting-room, and Stella breathed more freely when left alone. She could not be sure, of course, whether Ross had been attempting to "pump" her, or merely making talk. His motive in all probability had been mere curiosity—a vice not necessarily dangerous, although it is said to have by tradition killed a cat; an animal, too, credited by the same authority with extreme tenacity of life.

Stella was sure, from various indications, that Ross was not in Truscott's confidence, in matters outside of the department where Ross's duties lay, though here she saw no evidences of distrust on her employer's part. It seemed to her that if Truscott had desired Ross to know of his plans, he would himself have informed him; and that, the contrary being true, he wished him to be kept ignorant of them. At any rate, she was bound to secrecy. Stella sighed with regret. If her own father had been equally careful! Truscott had the wisdom of the serpent.

Ross returned to the subject several times, during the day. Stella made amends for her first slip by parrying every attack, in such a manner she fondly believed, as to throw even the astute Ross off the track.

But Ross was an old hand. That evening he was the last to leave the office. As soon as he was left alone, he went into the private office and tried Mr. Truscott's desk, but found it locked. He tried the knob of the safe, to see if perchance it had been left unfastened. Stella's desk in the next room was subjected to as close a scrutiny, but with no greater success.

"All of which goes to prove," soliloquized Ross, "that there is something important in the wind. Things of no value are not locked up so carefully. Let me see, where else can I look? Ah, yes, the waste-basket!"

He carried the waste-basket from the private office into the main office, emptied it on the floor by his own desk, and before returning it to its place by Truscott's desk, transferred to it the contents of his own waste-basket.

He repeated this process with Stella's basket, replacing its contents, merely as a matter of extreme precaution, with the waste-paper from a desk in the main office.

"It will take me some time to go through this," he muttered, looking down at the pile. "It's larger than usual. I'll take it home and examine it at my leisure."

He gathered up the papers and shuffled them together into a parcel, around which he put a couple of stout rubber bands, slipping the parcel into his pocket. In the evening, at home, he looked carefully through the mass, scanning each paper closely, but found nothing to enlighten him on the subject of his investigations.

When Ross had finished his examination of the waste paper, he lit a bad cigar, and, as he smoked it, indited the following note, addressed to an officer of the principal concern competing with the Truscott Company:—

"Dear Sir:—I am unable to report anything definite as yet. The excitement, the haste and the secrecy still continue. Everything is locked up tight, and not a scrap of information of any kind, bearing on the matter on foot, is discoverable. I have learned one fact, however—that a very large increase in the volume of the business is shortly to take place.

"The only person in the office who is entirely in T's confidence is his stenographer, a Miss Smith, who boards at No. 17 Oak Street. T. is thoroughly infatuated with her, and trusts her with everything. She is close as a clam around the office, but a mine of information, if you can find any one skilful enough to work it. It might at least pay to do a little prospecting. I think she is suspicious of me and I would suggest that she could be more easily approached by some one apparently disinterested. Meanwhile, I shall keep my eyes open and, as usual report as often as I have anything worth communicating."

Having read over this effusion, Ross enclosed it in a plain envelope, which having addressed and stamped, he deposited in the nearest letter-box. The remainder of the evening he spent in various disreputable haunts where he left a great deal more money than a man of his salary could afford to spend.

When Stella went to the supper table on the evening of the following day, she was introduced to a new boarder.

"Miss Smith," said her landlady, "let me make you acquainted with the latest addition to our family, Miss Pearce. Miss Pearce, Miss Smith."

Stella shook hands with the new boarder, a tall young woman with yellow hair and keen gray eyes, who greeted Stella cordially.

"*So* glad to know you, Miss Smith! Mrs. Greenacre has told me all about you. Before engaging board, I inquired about the other boarders, and when she said there was a stenographer among them, I decided at once to come here. I'm a bookkeeper, you know, and it's the dearest ambition of my life to learn shorthand. It would be so delightful to room with a stenographer! Mrs. Greenacre did not know whether you would care"—

Miss Pearce paused parenthetically, but Stella did not seize the opportunity presented. For obvious reasons she wished to be alone, and was indeed annoyed somewhat at the increase in the household. She had selected Mrs. Greengage's boarding-house because of the small number of boarders.

"But when I learned," continued Miss Pearce smoothly, "that I could have the room next to that of a stenographer, who was at the same time a person of culture and refinement—I do so dearly love culture and refinement!—I felt

(***** two manuscript pages missing here *****)

learned much that subsequently proved useful to her. She brought up old note-books from time to time, and dictated business letters to Miss Pearce, who proved an apt pupil. She did not write quite the same shorthand as Stella, but a different variation of the parent system devised by the late Sir Isaac Pitman.

"How funny your notes look," she would exclaim sometimes, looking over Stella's books. "But I suppose mine seem just as queer to you. I don't believe I could read one word of yours in ten."

Then she would blunder along, picking out here and there that she could read with apparent difficulty.

"How lovely it would be," she exclaimed one evening, "if we could go over our daily work together! It would be real business experience! I'll open a set of books for you, and give you, every evening, our transactions for the day as I have entered them at the office, and you can dictate letters to me like those you have written. Won't that be nice?"

"Why, yes," assented Stella, "that will be fine." It seemed like an eminently practical suggestion.

Miss Pearce promptly carried out her part of the proposed plan. Stella in turn dictated to her friend every evening certain letters. But Stella never again lost sight of Truscott's admonition of secrecy, and while Miss Pearce knew nothing about the oil business, and would therefore be unable to connect or recognize the importance of detached pieces of information, Stella nevertheless felt it best to be on the safe side, and carefully avoided the subject of the new enterprise, in the letters she dictated to Miss Pearce, as a still further precaution changing names and dates and details of the business, and substituting others that would answer equally well for business practice.

At the end of several weeks Stella was informed one evening that Miss Pearce had been called out of town to attend the death of a near relative. She left her regards for Miss Smith. During their brief association Stella had learned a great deal about the theory of bookkeeping. What knowledge Miss Pearce had acquired of shorthand, or other matters, Stella was not to learn until later.

XXIII.

The volume of correspondence in regard to the new enterprise kept Stella so busily employed that for some time she only perfunctorily footed the daily statements turned in by Mr. Ross and handed to her for checking. When there came a lull of a day or two in the letter-writing, she gave them a little more attention. These statements were in the nature of daily reports of accounts payable, and were drawn up merely for Mr. Truscott's information between the quarterly balance sheets. Stella had gone over the items for several consecutive days, when a second time she became obscurely conscious of something wrong. An examination of the statements for a week back, revealed no discrepancy, but Stella was still unsatisfied. But there was nothing on which to base a definite complaint to Mr. Truscott, and she would not risk the mortification of having her doubts declared groundless.

"If I were a better bookkeeper," she thought, "I could put my finger on the place; or, if I could see Mr. Ross's books, I believe I could find it now."

It was on a Saturday that Stella became aware of these perturbations in the orbit of Ross's system of accounts. So strong was her impression that it soon became a fixed idea, which weighed upon her mind all day, and even at night would not be dismissed. She went to bed early, but lay awake until long after midnight, running over in her mind the various hypotheses by which to account for her suspicion. When she finally fell asleep, it was to dream that she had examined Ross's books and discovered glaring irregularities. So vivid was the dream that she awoke to find herself trembling with excitement, but unable to recall the slightest detail of what had the moment before seemed so clear.

She went to church next morning, and all through the service footed columns of figures and balanced debits against credits. It occurred to her too, while the minister was reading the prayers, that Sunday afternoon would be an excellent time to examine Ross's books and compare them with the last few statements. Stella had been brought up to respect the Sabbath, but with stress laid upon the idea that the Sabbath was made for man and not man for the Sabbath; and she thought it could not be wrong to spend an hour of it in serving her employer by ferreting out a fraud. It was a fair application of the parable of pulling one's neighbor's ox out of a pit. The confidence reposed in her by Truscott had unconsciously moderated Stella's opinions of her employer, and the thought that she might do something to please him gave her a thrill of pleasure which she ascribed to the mere approbation of conscience for duty performed. She would not have admitted to herself any other possible reason for her interest in the affairs of one who had wronged her family so deeply.

It was easy for Stella to act upon this idea. The El Dorado Building was only a pleasant walk from her boarding-house. The only drawback was that the elevators were not run on Sunday afternoons. The toilsome journey up seven flights was not a pleasing prospect, but was offset by the consideration that this fact would probably leave the office deserted. The clerks, she had learned from Johnnie, sometimes went down on Sunday mornings, to catch up their work or kill time in a familiar place, but Stella had never heard of any one's being there on Sunday afternoons. She had a key to the outer office, and with the coast clear, she could make a careful examination of the books for the past month. If Ross had been manipulating the accounts fraudulently, she would discover the fact; if he had not, her mistake would be equally apparent. In either event her mind would be relieved, and in the latter case she would no longer be harboring unjust suspicions towards a fellow-clerk.

Stella left her boarding-house about two o'clock, and after ten minutes walk found herself at the El Dorado Building. The hall was deserted, though an open door in a corner, through which she could see a steep downward flight of stairs, suggested that the watch-man in charge had descended to some subterranean locality. Stella felt relieved at his absence; the length of her stay in the office was less likely to be noticed, and there would be less danger of interruption.

She had never before climbed the stairs to the office, and in her excitement it seemed a trifling exertion to mount the broad flight of marble steps stretching upward before her. Coming to the city from a small town, she had not yet ceased to be impressed by the costly magnificence of great modern buildings. Her feeling was one of sympathy, however, rather than of awe. She felt quite in harmony with the delicately veined white marble on which she trod, and with the polished bronze rail surmounting the artistic scroll-work of the balustrade. She recognized the bronze figure on the newel-post at the turn of the stairs as a copy of a famous statue in a foreign museum. Looking past it to the upper landing, her eye found new pleasure in the fresco on the wall. The artist had shed over a somewhat hackneyed theme, "Commerce Conquering the World" a glow of artistic fancy, and had carried the mind away from rum and oil and tobacco and hides and tallow to the ideal of a beautiful spirit emptying a horn of plenty over a smiling landscape. It seemed to Stella that this was her proper environment, to live surrounded by works of art, and the fruits of culture.

She climbed the first three flights of stairs with ease. At the fourth the muscular exertion began to tell upon her, and she stopped to rest; not too long, however, for her task might occupy several hours and she must get at it as soon as possible.

Stella resumed her upward march. She found it necessary to pause now at each floor, not so much for lack of breath as to rest the muscles subjected to so unusual a strain. Once she stepped to the window near the stair and looked out. It had been cloudy when she came into the building. Now the rain had begun to fall in a monotonous drizzle that promised to outlast the afternoon. The loneliness of the deserted building, the gloom without, the weariness of the long climb, would have depressed the spirits of one in an ordinary frame of mind; but Stella's mood this afternoon rendered her proof against any but pleasant impressions. She trembled as she drew near the office, lest it might be occupied, and her efforts be for naught. A slight sense of danger lent zest to the adventure. She had no scruples to combat. Her task was a righteous one, and had the approval of her conscience. She was doing her duty—the duty of the moment. Whatever her grievance against Mr. Truscott might be, it was clearly incumbent upon her to do well the work she had in hand. If her present expedition was not directly a part of her work, it was closely related thereto. The distinction was too fine to cause her any uneasiness.

Stella tried the door. It was locked. She took out her key, and having entered the office, locked the door again from the inside. She would thus be secure, at least from unauthorized intrusion.

The books were kept in a certain compartment or cupboard at the side of Ross's desk in the counting room. This cupboard was not locked, and, opening it, Stella found the particular ledger she wished to examine, a bulky volume, which only with an effort could she lift to the top of the desk. She then procured from her own desk the statements of the preceding week, and began her comparison. The ledger entries seemed correct, but Stella was conscious of something wrong. Again and again she went over the figures, checking each item with painstaking exactitude.

Suddenly the whole scheme of defalcation flashed before her mind. It was an old trick—though Stella did not know that,—as old as the hills; a juggling of figures by which countless bookkeepers have betrayed their trust and paved the way to ultimate detection and exposure. It was a scheme only possible where, through carelessness or over-confidence, the keeping of accounts and the handling of money were left in the same hands. An experienced accountant, going over the books would have discovered it in half the time Stella had taken. To her it seemed a wonderful piece of villainy, and Ross a very prince of defaulters. She was not able in the time at her disposal, to ascertain the extent of the shortage; but a hurried computation disclosed that in the last few weeks it amounted to about twenty thousand dollars. That so large a sum could be taken without exciting suspicion, was due to the fact that the accounts of the company were rendered quarterly, the larger collections extending over several weeks. Under this system a shortage of receipts would not be noticeable until the collection period had expired.

It occurred to Stella, while still absorbed in these calculations, that if some one should by chance come to the office, it might be well for her to have some ostensible reason for being there. A plausible excuse would be that she had come to complete some pressing work left unfinished on Saturday. She closed the ledger mechanically, and going into her room, removed her hat and laid it on the table, raised the lid of her desk, and spread a note-book open beside the typewriter.

While thus engaged she heard footsteps approaching along the hallway. For a moment she held her breath. Perhaps it was a tenant going to some other office, or the watchman on his rounds through the building. But the footsteps paused at the door to the Truscott Company's office, and she heard the click of a key in the lock.

Stella instinctively looked around for a point from which she might watch the newcomer while herself remaining invisible. If it were one of the ordinary clerks, the preparations she had just made would account for her presence. If it were her employer, it would be a convenient opportunity to make known her discovery. It turned out to be neither. As Stella peeped from behind the half-open door where she had partly hidden herself, the well known form of Ross entered the door and locked it behind him.

Stella was seized by a wild, uncontrollable terror. She had never liked this man, and had shown her aversion so clearly that he must have noticed it. She was locked in the office with him, all alone in a great building, entirely at his mercy if he should choose to injure her. That he was a man of lax principles she had always suspected: from her brother's letter she had learned that he was a gambler; and she had just ascertained beyond question that he was a thief. She had left his book lying on the desk. If he should learn of her presence and surmise her errand, he might be desperate enough to kill her in the interests of his own safety. She trembled and turned pale at these thoughts, and looked wildly around for some adequate place of concealment. There was no outlet except the door, which was in full view from almost every part of the office. The clothes-press seemed to offer the best hiding-place. It was quite large enough to hold her, and unless the bookkeeper's suspicions should be aroused she might stay hidden there until he should have gone away.

Ross had directed his steps toward his own desk, so that Stella had only a moment to act while his back was turned to her. She snatched up her hat and sprang into the clothes-press. She drew the door lightly to,—it fortunately made no noise,—and left a slight crack, through which she could get air to breathe and at the same time have a field of vision large enough to take in Ross's probable movements.

When the bookkeeper saw the ledger lying on the desk, he, in his turn, started and turned pale. Had Stella had any lingering doubt of his guilt, his manner would have removed it. He turned and swept the office with a suspicious glance.

"Did I leave that book on the desk?" he asked himself audibly. "I *have* done such a thing, but I could almost swear that I put it away last night."

Stella watched him through the narrow slit. He opened the ledger, turned over the leaves, scanning them closely, until he found what Stella had for a moment forgotten,— the slip of paper containing her memorandum of his stealings.

Stella from her hiding place saw him pick up the piece of paper. When, after glancing at it, he turned his head and swept the office with his eyes, her heart sank with terror at the expression of mingled fear and hate that disfigured his countenance. With bated breath she watched him slip the memorandum into his pocket and start toward the room where she was concealed. Up to the discovery of the fateful slip Ross had not suspected that any one was present in the office. But the instinct of self-preservation impelled him to look. He had recognized Stella's figures, and when he saw the open desk, and the note-book lying beside the uncovered typewriter, he realized that she had been there recently. True to the instinct of treachery, he seized the note-book and thrust it into his pocket.

Stella might still have escaped discovery, had not Ross suddenly become conscious of the perfume of violets, a bunch of which Stella had worn fastened at her throat. Ross's extremity of danger rendered his senses preternaturally acute. He stood in a listening attitude, sniffing the air with distended nostrils, for all the world like a wild beast following his prey or seeking to elude his pursuers. Stella's heart throbbed furiously; surely, she felt, he must be able to hear it beating.

With cat-like tread Ross moved toward the front the office, and passed beyond Stella's line of vision. Not daring to change her position, she waited in terrified suspense for several minutes—the time seemed an hour to her strained nerves—and then a heavy weight came suddenly against the door of her hiding-place, and the key was immediately turned in the lock. Stella felt the wardrobe moving upon its castors. She shrieked in vague terror, and then swooning, knew no more.

XXIV.

Stella, upon regaining consciousness, found herself in the dark. Whether night had fallen or not she had no means of knowing, nor could she imagine how many hours she had lain there. With consciousness her terror returned, and she screamed and beat her hands against the sides of her narrow prison. But in a few moments her calmer judgment resumed its sway, and she began to study the situation. She had undoubtedly been locked up for some little time. She need fear no bodily harm from Ross, for he had locked her up merely to secure time for his own escape. The clothes-press, of which she had felt such an unreasoning terror, had saved her life; but for its presence, Ross might have resorted to violence to gain the time he had so easily secured by locking her up. In all reasonable probability she would not be able to escape before morning, by which time any act of violence would have been discovered, to the great increase of Ross's peril.

Stella tried the door. It did not move. She tried it again, bracing herself against the back of the clothes-press and bringing all her strength to bear. It resisted her efforts at first, but finally yielded. She heard the lock crack. The fastenings gave way; the door moved outward about three inches, and—stopped.

It was near nightfall, as Stella now perceived, but she could not see what obstructed the outward movement of the door. Putting out her hand to feel, it came in contact with a cold hard, smooth surface, very much like iron. She peered through the opening, and ran her hand once or twice up and down the barrier, before fully grasping the situation. The iron safe, she knew, stood near a corner, leaving about two feet between it and the wall. Into this space Ross, after turning the key on Stella, had pushed the clothes-press;—being on rollers, a strong man could move it with some effort, and Ross at that moment could have moved mountains. It filled the space so completely as to prevent the opening of the door for more than a handsbreadth, while the wall would equally prevent escape if the prisoner should by any possibility succeed in breaking through the thin panels at the back of the clothes-press.

Stella realized the apparent hopelessness of her position, and was in despair. The prospect of spending the night in this dungeon would have appalled a stouter heart. She put her wits to work to devise some means of escape.

She tried the ends of the wardrobe, but they were stout and did not yield in the least to her efforts. She had read somewhere of a young man, inadvertently locked up in one of a ship's water-tight compartments, who had finally attracted attention to his dangerous plight by pounding with his shoe upon the iron lining of the vessel. Stella drew off one of her small shoes and hammered with the heel upon the end of the wardrobe, in the faint hope that some passing janitor or watchman might hear her from the corridor. But her efforts proved unavailing, and she finally sank exhausted to the floor.

"I'll try the top," she thought with a sudden inspiration, after resting a while.

There were several packages of stationery lying on the bottom of the clothes-press. By piling these one upon another she was able to reach and push against the top of the wardrobe. To her joy it yielded—not a great deal, for her position did not permit her to exert much of an upward pressure—but enough to indicate that the top was not securely fastened down, but held in place, at least in part, by its own weight. With renewed hope and energy Stella groped about her prison until she found a slight projection upon which to rest one foot, the pile of packages supporting the other. This gave her a good lifting leverage, and by pushing with all her might—she would not have judged herself capable of so much exertion—she raised one side of the top until it fell over upon the safe below with a crash loud enough to be faintly audible even to the distant watchman in the entrance lobby. He supposed the wind was slamming one of the ventilators in the roof, and did not look up from the Sunday paper.

Nothing now remained between Stella and liberty but a rather awkward climb. She was young and active, and there were no spectators to embarrass her. Before long she found herself on top of the safe, from which she descended without much difficulty to the floor below, with no greater injury than the loss of several small pieces of cuticle.

It was night, but there was light enough for Stella to faintly distinguish objects in the office. When she reached the floor she remembered that she had left her shoe and her hat in the clothes-press. She laid hold of the piece of furniture to draw it out from behind the safe; but the reaction from her extraordinary exertions had already begun; her strength was not sufficient, and she was compelled to give up the effort. She would not for the world have climbed back into the wardrobe. There was no alternative but to go without these ordinarily necessary parts of street attire. She closed her desk, groped her way to the door, and unlocked it, drawing a breath of relief as she noted the dim lights in the lower halls of the building, from which a faint radiance rose to where Stella stood. She flew rather than walked down the stairs, at some risk of falling; and in but little more than a minute she had covered the seven flights and found herself in the entrance lobby.

The watchman looked up in surprise as she descended the last flight. It was unusual, to say the least, for a woman to be in the block at such an hour on Sunday. But her face was familiar, and he recognized her right to be there. He tipped his hat. She nodded in response and hurried out. It was raining— the cheerless drizzle of three or four hours before. There was a hood or porch over the door, and she stood under this for a moment while wondering what was best for her to do next.

"How shall I notify Mr. Truscott?" she asked herself. Her own safety being assured, the realization of Ross's crime, and that he had been warned in time to escape, returned with redoubled force.

"If I take a street-car, I shall attract attention because I have no hat. If I walk, it will take too long, and I have but one shoe."

A taxicab stood in front of a neighboring club-house. She had no money, but the cabman could be paid at the other end of his course. She crossed the street, feeling a weird sensation of discomfort as her stockinged foot splashed into a pool of cold water.

"Is this a public cab?" she asked.

"Yes'm," said the cabman.

He sprang down from his seat and threw the door open obsequiously.

Stella stepped into the carriage. "Drive to 650 Oakwood Avenue," she said.

"Mr. Truscott's, mum?"

"Yes. And hurry, please."

The cabby closed the door, climbed to his seat, whipped up his horses, and started off at a good pace—not too fast, however, for the distance was short, and he wished to seem to have done something to earn his fare. Nevertheless, the carriage reached its destination in a few minutes. The driver, who was evidently familiar with the location, turned into the driveway leading back to the house, which like all the residences on the north side of the street, stood back several rods from the sidewalk. The wheels crunched on the gravelled path, and the carriage drew up before the front entrance.

Stella turned the handle of the carriage door and sprang out before the coachman could dismount to assist her.

"Wait," she said, "I shall want you further."

She had grasped the old-fashioned knocker, and was about to bring it down sharply, when she espied an electric push-button at one side of the door and let the knocker return to the repose from which it was rarely disturbed. A push at the button was soon answered. The face that appeared in the door was the familiar one of Mr. Truscott's valet, George, whom she had often seen at the office.

"Why, it's Miss Smith!" he exclaimed, in some surprise, which was quite excusable in view of the unexpected visit, the unusual hour and the somewhat agitated, not to say disordered appearance of the young woman confronting him.

"Yes, it is I, George," she answered. "Is Mr. Truscott at home?"

"Yes, 'm, he's home."

"Tell him, please, that I should like to see him at once."

"Yas 'm. But walk in, Miss Smith, and sed-down till I calls 'im."

He ushered Stella into the reception room adjoining the entrance hall. She sank into a capacious armchair. Left alone for several minutes, she looked around her curiously. Her growing interest in this man,—an interest she did not stop to analyze, but which, taking its rise in repulsion, had been complicated by a compelled admiration of Truscott's extraordinary executive talents,—led her to notice instinctively the things that made up his personal environment. She knew already that he kept bachelor's hall, with a staff of servants consisting of a cook, a coachman and a valet. If she had known nothing of his household whatever, she would have gathered, from the lack of certain accessories, the absence of refined womanhood in the household. The room was comfortably, even elegantly furnished with a Persian rug on the floor, several choice paintings on the walls, and handsome tables and chairs, not of the latest designs. But a certain masculine angularity betrayed itself even in the attitudes of the furniture. One side of the room was almost filled by a book-case with a glass front. Stella had scarcely time to more than glance at the titles and bindings, but perceived that the books represented the more serious and solid side of literature. Beside a volume of Shakespeare up on the table stood a bronze smoker's tray of fantastic design; while over the wide marble mantel, which was in keeping with the old-fashioned interior, a pair of spreading antlers suggested wide forest reaches, baying hounds, and the excitement of the chase. A subtle masculine influence seemed to emanate from the room; and impressed Stella, much as did Truscott's presence, with a sense of his power,—a power to which, with her knowledge of his past, she would have shrunk from trusting herself so long, had it not been for the sacred nature of her great task. Her conduct on this particular day she ascribed to nothing more than common honesty. This man was paying for her services, in the course of which she had seen him being imposed upon. To do otherwise than warn him promptly would have been only less culpable than to participate in the crime itself. And Stella, she proudly felt, was the very embodiment of honesty.

Through one open wing of a sliding-door she caught a glimpse of a spacious dining-room, wainscoted in dark oak. A massive sideboard of the same wood was visible, as well as a ponderous chandelier above a polished oaken table with carved legs of an antique pattern. Stella had time to wonder, even in the few minutes of her waiting, whether Truscott had bought the house furnished, or whether his own taste had so perfectly adapted the appointments to its plan and style.

Mr. Truscott entered the room from the hall, his usually inscrutable face revealing a little of the surprise that his servant had manifested, but better controlled and less obvious.

"Why, good evening, Miss Smith," he said, advancing with extended hand. "This is an unexpected pleasure."

Stella rose, and mechanically placed her hand in his. Even in her embarrassment she was struck by the courtesy of his greeting and the gentleness of his manner. In his own home he seemed quite a different man from the stern autocrat of the counting-room.

"Good evening, sir. I came to see you"—

Truscott had noted her somewhat dishevelled appearance. So occupied had Stella been with other thoughts that she had forgotten for a moment to think of herself. She knew her head was bare, but was not aware that her hair was disordered, that there were several patches on her face where, in her acrobatic escape from the clothes-press, she had come in contact with accumulations of dust. Mr. Truscott observed these things, and that the girl was laboring under some excitement that lent additional glow to her cheeks and sparkle to her eyes, and seemed to define more strongly certain characteristic lines, indicative, he was pleased to think, of courage, high purpose, and invincible honesty. What her business might be, he could not even imagine, but he felt sure it would be nothing inconsistent with these qualities.

"You are in trouble," he said. "Tell me all about it."

"No," she answered, "I'm not in trouble, at least not on my own account, though I was in some distress a few minutes ago. I came to tell you about something that concerns your interests. The bookkeeper, Mr. Ross, has been robbing the company, and is some twenty thousand dollars short in his accounts."

Mr. Truscott manifested less surprise than Stella had anticipated. She could see his expression change from that of masculine sympathy for distressed womanhood to the cold, hard mask of the keen man of business, alert in the protection of his own interests, accustomed to human guile in many phases, and expert in circumventing it.

"Yes," he said "I have no doubt that is true. I can see, in the light of the accomplished fact, that he was quite capable of it. How long have you known this?"

"Since three o'clock."

"How did you learn it?"

"From the books."

"Is he aware of your knowledge?"

"He is."

"How long has he known that you knew it?"

"Since four o'clock."

"Ah! He has had three hours warning. A man can go a long way in three hours."

"But he thinks my mouth is closed until morning," said Stella.

"Indeed! Then perhaps you had better tell me all about it, and then we shall be in a better position to consider what course to follow."

Stella then detailed with considerable animation the events of the afternoon, recurring also to the former occasion when she had discovered a discrepancy. Truscott followed with the closest attention her description of the visit to the office, the discovery of the defalcation, the arrival of Ross, her imprisonment, and her escape. He listened in silence, except for an occasional question to expedite the narrative or ascertain the precise nature of the false entries by which the defalcation had been covered up. The man of business, robbed by his trusted servant, took entire possession of his mind, to the momentary exclusion of the fair face and lithe form of the young woman seated before him. For the time being she was no more in his eyes than a telegram, or a business letter, or the unseen interlocutor at the other end of a telephone line—she was simply a source of knowledge, a medium of communication, of no possible sort of consequence as compared to the message brought.

When she had finished, he made no acknowledgment of the service rendered; and events hurried along so rapidly that Stella did not notice the omission; indeed, it was quite in keeping with her original conception of his character, which time had only slightly modified. He touched the bell that stood upon the table, and George appeared as suddenly as the genii summoned by Aladdin's lamp.

"Bring me a railroad guide."

It was there in a moment. He turned the leaves rapidly.

"There have been only two trains out of Groveland since four o'clock," he said; "one was over the B. C. & A. to Huntley, where there are no through connections until morning; the other was an east-bound train, and the chances are three to one that he would go west. The next train out of town is the Chicago express at seven-thirty. We have twenty-five minutes to notify the police and have the station watched."

"There is a cab at the door," said Stella, "the one in which I came. May I ask you to pay the driver?—I had n't the money and I could n't walk."

"Certainly. As there is no time to lose, I will take your carriage, and I'll ask you to wait until my own can be brought round to take you home; it will be only a few minutes. I'll do what I can to head off this thief. In the meantime, Miss Smith," he added, extending his hand, "I shall not forget what we owe to your foresight and courage, nor what you have undergone in the company's service. Good-bye—until morning."

Stella heard the cab roll away swiftly. Five minutes later George announced that Mr. Truscott's carriage was ready, and in five minutes more Stella found herself upon her own street. She requested the coachman to let her out at the corner—the carriage would have attracted attention by drawing up at her boarding-house door. Because of the rain, which was still falling, fortunately the usual summer group was absent from the porch. The hall door stood open, and Stella was able to gain her room unobserved.

When she found herself safe, with the dangers and perplexities of the day at an end, the tension of her overwrought nerves relaxed and she sank utterly exhausted upon her bed. An hour later, however, she crawled downstairs long enough to get a cup of tea and say that she had been lying down and had not cared for supper. Then she went to bed and slept a sleep broken now and then by dreams and nervous starts which showed how profoundly she had been moved by the rapid and dramatic events of the afternoon.

XXV.

Ross got safely away for the time being. The agencies set in operation by Truscott to find him were unavailing, and many months elapsed before he was finally located in a certain South American country with which at that time the United States had no treaty of extradition. In the meantime events involving Stella's mission and Truscott's great scheme moved rapidly toward a decisive culmination. An expert accountant straightened out the books of the company in a few days. Whether Ross had been able, by supplying the enemy with information, to injure his employer, was not yet apparent. Truscott supposed him entirely ignorant of his recent plans, and Stella did not attach a great deal of importance to his theft of her letter-book, since Ross, she knew, could not read her short-hand notes. A new bookkeeper was installed in the vacant place, and the business of the office went on in the usual, or rather the extraordinary way, in which it had been conducted for the past few weeks.

While there was no pronounced change in Truscott's manner toward Stella, he now always spoke to her in the morning, when he passed through her room to reach his own, and she thought she detected in his greeting a shade of deference not apparent before her recent experience. The difference was slight, but it gave Stella a thrill of elation. She knew that iron did not bend easily; and the fact that it bent at all was evidence that considerable force had been applied. She thought Truscott the least impressionable of men; it was a triumph to have moved him, however slightly.

Stella's views in regard to the unmasking of Truscott's early misdeeds had been imperceptibly modified. At first she had seen exposure coming swiftly, like a thunderbolt, or the wrath of God, striking the usurper from his pedestal and covering him with well-merited obloquy. Now she thought of the great event as merely a retribution. Instead of an avenging fury driving the sinner to ruin, she would stand to him in the attitude of a calm and reproachful goddess. Remorse should be his portion. She would demand nothing of him but what he had taken; she would not ruin or embarrass him by exposure. She would be his conscience. Knowing her as he would, the mere consciousness of her disapproval, her scorn, her knowledge of his wrong-doing, would be as great a punishment as any public scandal could inflict. Neither did the urgency of the affair seem quite so great as at first. The longer she remained near him, the more thoroughly Truscott would know her, the higher would be his opinion of her character, the greater would be his remorse, and therefore the more severe his punishment.

Stella, however, while the chief actor, was not the moving spirit in this matter of discovery and restitution. Mrs. Merwin could not have entered into Stella's thoughts, if they had been imparted to her. She saw in the situation not a good or a great man who had taken one false step as yet unretracted, but an unscrupulous, crafty villain, who had robbed her husband and condemned his widow and orphans to poverty. Whether he suffered remorse or not was no concern of hers. She wanted her own, and if she could have seen the despoiler endure a day of disgrace for every day of her own humiliation, she would have felt that justice was far from done. Her husband's life could not be restored; the vindication of his good name at this late day could never entirely compensate for the long years during which his memory had rested under a cloud. She was spared the knowledge that for all but a few old acquaintances, his name had long since been forgotten.

For a week or more Mrs. Merwin had not been pleased with the tone of Stella's letters. They were too few, and did not report sufficient progress. Mrs. Merwin determined to bring events to a crisis, if possible. With this end in view, she wrote Stella the following letter:

"Dear Stella:—

    "I had a dream last night, so vivid that it seemed more like reality. I believe, Stella, that it was something more than a dream—it was a prophetic vision. In it I lived over again all my years of happiness with your dear father, and the dark days when trouble came, and the last sad hours before his eyes were closed and his kind voice stilled forever. 'Do not weep, dear Alice,' he said again—the words are burned into my memory— 'I have made a sad mess of it, but Wendell will see that you are provided for. Trust in him. He has papers that will make everything clear, and show what has become of my property.'

"I awoke with a terrible pain at my heart, and thought, for a little while, that I should join my dear husband sooner than I had expected, and before I had seen our great trust executed. Stella, I cannot stand this suspense much longer! I have not the strength. Another such attack will carry me off; and I could not rest in my grave with my dearest wish ungratified.

"Dear Stella, if you have any respect for your poor father's memory, if you love your mother, if you wish to place your brother beyond the reach of temptation, do not put off your duty any longer! Look for your father's papers; I am convinced that if you seek them diligently they will come to light. Do not write to me again until you have done something; I can bear your silence better than disappointment. Again I beseech you, Stella, by your father's memory, by your mother's love, do something, and do it soon! Until then I shall remain,

"Your unhappy mother,
"Alice Merwin."

Such an appeal could lead to but one result—action. Stella received this letter on Saturday afternoon. She determined to make another Sunday visit to the office and examine the contents of the safe. She knew that her employer intended spending the day in the country, and that she need fear no interruption from him. While she had not forgotten her former experience, and did not relish a second Sunday visit to the office, she was brave enough to undertake it. She was not likely to be disturbed, and Sunday afternoon was her only opportunity to make the thorough search that would probably be required.

But Stella's night was not a pleasant one. She felt unaccountable reluctance to take the decisive step upon which she had resolved. She knew it was her duty, not merely to herself, but to her mother and her brother and, above all, to her dead father's memory. Had she alone been concerned, she felt that she might even have let her rights go by default, rather than to do that which grew more and more distasteful as she approached it.

XXVI.

Stella felt strangely depressed as she climbed the stairs of the El Dorado Building on Sunday afternoon. She had not gone to church in the morning; why, she had not asked herself; probably because of some obscure incongruity between worship and the afternoon task to which she looked forward.

The day was bright and glorious, an ideal autumn day; but Stella, usually a very barometer in sensitiveness to atmospheric conditions, on this afternoon was proof against sunshine and cheerfulness. When she entered the hall of the building, the sight of the porter in the lobby made her feel guiltily uncomfortable, and she found herself wondering what dark speculations he might be making as to the object of her visit. On the former occasion she had mounted the stairs rapidly, and yet the time had seemed long ere she reached the top. Now, though her feet were heavy as lead, she seemed to ascend with great rapidity. The marble stairs and mosaic floors, for aught she noticed of them, might have been mildewed stone or crumbling brick; the frescoes on the wall were mere gaudy daubs in the light, mere blurs of color in the shadows. She was vividly conscious, took of this incongruity between her feelings and her mission. The chosen instrument to right a great wrong, her heart should have been fired with zeal, her feet clothed with wings. On the contrary, the nearer she approached it, the more her duty seemed like martyrdom. She fought against this reluctance, and while combatting it successfully, the struggle was keen enough to render her supremely uncomfortable.

She unlocked and locked again behind her the office door. She then laid off her hat, removed her gloves, put on her office apron, which she took from the clothes-press, thus composing herself for an afternoon's work, and at the same time deferring it as long as possible. She then attempted to open the safe. Several times she failed, but finally the combination worked and the ponderous door swung open. The hinges needed oiling, and emitted a discordant creak which seemed almost uncanny and made Stella shiver in an ecstacy of discomfort.

The safe was not of the most modern design, and was used almost solely as a repository for Truscott's personal papers and memoranda, there being a vault in the counting-room for the company's books and the current cash. There were compartments for books, pigeon-holes for papers, and several drawers, one of which, as she had often noticed, was locked. Stella reasoned that in this drawer would be found the papers of which her father had spoken; but the book accounts and memoranda bearing upon Truscott's conduct in the matter would more likely be in the open compartments; and to these she first directed her attention.

Beginning at the upper left-hand pigeon-hole, she worked her way systematically, through the upper horizontal tier, then taking the others in turn. For a while her search revealed nothing that could throw light upon the subject of her inquiry. The contents of the safe had plainly been arranged by a person of an orderly mind. Papers of various kinds, receipts, letters, check-stubs, copies of contracts, and so forth, were filed in chronological order, and neatly tied with red tape. Stella scanned each paper carefully. As soon as she saw that it had no bearing upon her mission, she laid it scrupulously aside; she had no desire to pry into Mr. Truscott's affairs further than they concerned her own.

The afternoon wore away, and still Stella had not found what she sought. Had she chosen, she might, from the data before her, have studied the whole development of Wendell Truscott's career; and in spite of herself she could not fail to learn much of it. There were some things she did not understand, and did not try to, feeling that she had no right, though vaguely conscious that they were sometimes consistent, sometimes inconsistent, with her estimate of her employer's character.

During the two hours she had so far spent in examining the papers in the open compartments of the safe, she had found only one thing that might bear upon her own affairs. In a little package of check-stubs, she came across numerous memoranda of checks made to the order of Mahlon Fitch. The name was familiar, as that of her father's executor, who still had charge of the unsettled remnant of his estate. There was nothing in the checks, however, to connect them definitely with her father's business, and Stella merely made a memorandum of the dates and amounts. A vague suspicion crossed her mind, that perhaps they were a division of the spoil; a sop thrown to the jackal that he might not by his howling betray his master the lion, while the latter was gorging his prey! But this could only be determined when she should find the all-important papers.

As the minutes rolled on Stella became more and more certain that what she sought was to be found in the locked compartment. She had hoped to find it outside. What she had hitherto examined had been surrendered by the enemy, so to speak, for he had given her access to the safe. The locked compartment was another matter; it had not been opened to her. She knew that the key was kept in a drawer in Truscott's desk, for she had seen him take it out and use it. She realized that if she was to succeed in her search she must get it and unlock the drawer. From this step she had shrunk, and now only justified it by her mother's argument that Truscott having by his own course placed himself beyond the pale of ordinary rules of human conduct, had laid himself open to attack with any available weapon. There was no alternative; in no other way could she accomplish a righteous purpose. In such a case the end, she tried to convince herself, justified the means.

She opened the desk, found the key, and as she inserted it in the lock, felt herself in a whirl of conflicting emotions. One instant she feared she might not find the papers; if not, it would break her mother's heart, perhaps literally as well as figuratively. The next instant she was filled with dread lest she might find them—why, she did not stop to inquire.

She turned the key and pulled the little knob. Several neatly arranged packets of papers lay before her. The afternoon had grown cloudy and the hour late, and Stella drew the little drawer from its place and carried it over by the window where there was light enough to examine its contents. She lifted one bundle of papers, and under it saw another, on which was endorsed in Truscott's familiar handwriting, "Merwin Papers and Memoranda."

A wave of exultant feeling swept over her. Her hand trembled so with excitement, that she dropped the package on the floor, and had to stoop and pick it up. Her doubts and fears were momentarily swept away by the rush of emotion. Here at last must be the precious documents! The cloud would be lifted from her father's name, her mother's declining years would be spent in comfort and ease, and she, Stella, should take the place in society to which her birth, her talents and wealth, entitled her.

She untied the package, and unfolding one of the papers, saw that it was written in a fine hand, of which she had seen many specimens, and which she recognized as her father's. The clouds had grown thicker, the night was falling, and she could not see to read.

Pulling down the window-shades in order that the light might not attract attention from the outside, she turned the screw that switched on the current to the electric lamp. There was no responsive glow. The furnace fires were evidently out and the dynamo not running.

"I'll take them home with me," she said to herself. "They are ours, and I shall keep them. If I find anything here that does not belong to us, I can return it early in the morning, before Mr. Truscott arrives. If he misses the rest, he cannot inquire of me, for I shall not be here, when he comes; and the fact that the papers have been recovered will soon be brought to his attention."

She raised the shades, put the drawer back in its place, locked it, and shut the safe. Having returned to its place the key taken from Mr. Truscott's desk, she took off her apron, wrapped it in a piece of paper with some other little personal objects in the drawer of her desk, put on her hat as well as she could in the dusk, and left the office, drawing on her gloves as she went along the corridor. When she reached the entrance hall she astonished the watchman by greeting him with a radiant smile and remarking that it had been a lovely day.

XXVII.

The Country Club, where Truscott was engaged to dine on Sunday, was an organization of rather exclusive membership, recruited mostly from among elderly business men of large affairs. Two railroad presidents were numbered among the elect, one of whom, a bachelor of ample means, occupied, during the summer, an apartment in the club house. The dinner to which Truscott was invited was given by this gentleman, whose dinners, even in this temple of good living, were always worthy of attention.

The outward and visible shell housing this select company of reputed millionaires, was a spacious and beautiful structure of stone and brick and wood, located about five miles from the city, and reached by a fine macadamized road connecting with the city pavement at the municipal boundary. The clubhouse stood in a grove, on a high bluff, directly on the south shore of the lake. From the broad verandah running along three sides of the house, the eye could follow the curve of the shore until it was lost in the distance. To the left, the masts of the shipping in the city's harbor could be faintly made out, through the curtain of smoke, more or less dense, according to the wind and weather, from the intervening factories that supplied the members of the Country Club with the money they spent so freely. Artists might criticise, architects might deplore, visitors might gibe at, the inky pall that at times overhung an otherwise fair city; but to the men who frequented the Country Club this canopy sometimes dense, sometimes tenuous, now high in air, now hugging the earth, was a veritable pillar of cloud by day, and of fire by night, to lead these chosen children of fortune on their journey toward the promised land of pelf and power.

Not as many members of the club were to be seen on this particular day as usually drove out on pleasant Sunday afternoons. The clouds, which had threatened rain all the afternoon, had doubtless kept some away. Only a half dozen or so had been bidden to General Farwell's dinner, and these were received in his own apartments in the second story of the club-house.

There were present a couple of bankers, a well-known and popular lawyer, an iron manufacturer, a street railroad magnate, and several other men well known in financial circles. Every man among them had a business to which he gave his attention and from which he derived at least a part of his income. The West is still intolerant of the idle rich; the gentleman of leisure, pure and simple, the *dilettante* who dabbles in art or literature as a mere cloak for idleness, has not yet obtained a firm footing in the middle West. The only excuse for a life of leisure, west of New York, is to have acquired means as the result of a business career, and to have earned, at the approach of old age, the right to retire from active life; while even most of those thus qualified for retirement, retain some nominal tie with active life, such as the directorship of a bank or a railroad company.

"Truscott, I'm glad to see you," exclaimed the general, when his most youthful guest, and the last to arrive, came in.

"We were just talking about you, and what a wonderful run of luck you've had since you succeeded Merwin in the oil business."

"Thank you, general; I assure you it was mere luck."

"You're too modest, my boy! I did n't mean at all that it was mere luck. I know you've worked hard, and to good advantage. But many a poor devil has worked as diligently, and used excellent judgment; and just at the critical point in his career, some unforeseen calamity, entirely beyond his control, and beyond reasonable anticipation would come like a thunderclap and knock his prosperity into a cocked hat."

"I never saw a more striking illustration of that," said Mr. Dalton, "than the case of your predecessor, Merwin. By the way, that reminds me! The last time I spoke of him was to Matilda Wedderburn, a month ago, when I met her at your office. I promised to call on her—I really must. A most delightful woman!"

"I thought Wendell and Miss Wedderburn would have been running in double harness long ago," chipped in Major Darling, who was the sporting member of the party and owned a famous trotter.

Truscott colored slightly.

"I guess she's such a high stepper that it's hard for her to find a running mate," continued the Major.

"I've always thought," returned Mr. Dalton, "that Wendell and she were made for each other. But as I was saying," he continued, angling back to the original subject, for which Truscott felt grateful, "I never saw any worse luck. Merwin was in the full tide of success. He had a splendid business, a royal income, unlimited credit—every outward sign of prosperity, every promise of great development; and yet he was caught, and went under."

Truscott was looking out of the window.

"Gentlemen," he said, "Excuse me for a moment. There is a man in the yard to whom I wish to speak."

"Now that Truscott is n't here," continued Mr. Dalton, as the door closed, "I might add that I never quite understood Merwin's failure. True, he was caught in the panic of that year, like a lot of other fellows—I got pinched myself, but squeezed through all right—but I never saw how he had been hit hard enough to ruin him so completely; if everything was straight, there would have been a respectable fragment left when the worst was said about the panic. There was something mysterious about that failure, something that has never come to light, although there were some ugly rumors."

"Truscott was in the firm, was n't he?" asked one of the bankers, whose residence in the city dated back only some five years.

"No," said Mr. Dalton, "Wendell was only a clerk, though he stood pretty close to Merwin. He knew all about the business and bought it in when it was sold; I suppose he borrowed the money. He and the widow quarrelled afterwards, I never quite knew why."

"Speaking of the widow," said the Major, "she was a fine woman. What became of her? And there was a cub of a boy, and a very pretty little girl."

"The widow moved away somewhere, to some small town," said Mr. Dalton. "I suppose she has brought the boy up to be a clerk, and the girl to be a school-ma'am or a typewriter, or something of that sort."

"Speaking of typewriters," said the major, as Truscott came in again, "reminds me of a story Billy Fox was telling me about a girl that works in Tom Martin's office. She's a stunning blonde and"—

He went on with his story, which did not reflect any credit on either the narrator or any one else mentioned.

"This is a rather stupid party," said Truscott to himself. "They seem to select the most disagreeable subjects they can think of."

He resumed his seat by the window and smoked his cigar, but did not join in the laughter that followed the major's story. He had heard stories of a certain sort before, even worse ones than this; he never soiled his lips with them, but he had never felt quite so much disgusted at them as at this one.

"What an old brute that fellow is," he thought, "I don't really see why Farwell invites him here with gentlemen."

Truscott might have said something discourteous, had a diversion not been created by the announcement that dinner was served.

The dinner was above criticism. It was served in a room overlooking the lake. The appointments were the best that money could buy. The general was something of an epicure. The club's cook had been his own, and he had only relinquished his treasure on condition that he himself should have the choice of suites at the club, and the reversion of the *chef's* services during the winter, when the club-house was closed.

A clear turtle soup was swallowed in a silence more eloquent than words. Blue points on the half-shell led up to broiled blue-fish that melted in the mouth, and was washed down by sherry of a rare brand. Other courses followed, the whole forming a banquet fit for the gods, if the gods had been educated up to modern standards. Had Cleopatra been a genuine epicure, she would never have risked her digestion by swallowing a pearl dissolved in vinegar, when she might have swallowed the oyster whole in its own juice.

Conversation over the cigars took a turn toward shop. During an animated discussion of the business outlook, under a new presidential administration and a pending revision of existing tariff laws, Mr. Carlyle, one of the bankers, was called to the long distance telephone downstairs. He returned in about ten minutes, looking slightly troubled.

"I' ve just been talking with my correspondent in New York," he said, breaking abruptly into the conversation. "As I believe you are all stockholders in my bank, I may as well speak freely. My correspondent says there is a very uneasy feeling in Wall Street, or in the hotel lobbies and clubs that represent Wall Street on Sundays. Rumors are afloat in London that several large banking houses, interested in extensive schemes of colonial development, are seriously involved, and heavy failures are imminent."

Instantly the company were all attention. There was no one of them but had interests of greater or less magnitude, dependent, for their security, upon the maintenance of existing financial conditions—interests which any sudden disturbance of the money market would embarrass, temporarily if not seriously.

This announcement practically broke up the dinner party. Of them all Truscott seemed the least disturbed. Perhaps his comparative youth made him more sanguine. He remembered one panic, but he had been too poor at that time to be personally involved; indeed, his fortune dated from that time. His great enterprise was rapidly approaching a successful climax. In a day or two he would need to use large sums of money, both to meet maturing obligations and to secure important leases and contracts. But he did not anticipate any serious difficulty. Much of the needed funds were in the bank. His credit was of the best. He expected large remittances during the week. The recent defalcation of Ross had been merely a ripple on the surface of his affairs. He felt, in fact, too secure in his position to be embarrassed by anything short of a financial earthquake, and there was nothing in a temporary London flurry to portend such a catastrophe.

The suddenness of the panic that developed on the following morning was only equalled by its widespread and disastrous character. At the opening of banking hours in London the failure was announced of a great banking house, the strongest in Great Britain, except the Bank of England. The results of this failure recalled the familiar law of physics, commonly illustrated by a row of bricks on end, which knock each other down in turn when the first is toppled over against the next. An ordinary bank failure would have involved a few correspondents, a few depositors, a few commercial houses. But this one shook the whole financial fabric, for this house had stood like a rock for a hundred years. Its name was a synonym for security. So wide were its business ramifications that the failure directly involved an enormous number of institutions and individuals, all over the civilized world. It was itself, indeed, only an intermediate failure, for the collapse of a great colonial correspondent had brought down this financial monarch. Add to this the moral effect, upon the weak and the timid, of such a shock, and it is not strange that for a time the very springs of credit seemed dried up; business was demoralized and disaster and distrust reigned supreme.

Truscott was hard hit. The expected remittances did not come in; the banks from which he had meant to borrow would not lend; while the demands he anticipated, as well as others unlooked for, were made with a fierceness and persistency that revealed the extremity of his creditors, and their distrust of anything except cold cash. In addition to the difficulties which might be reasonably expected at such a juncture there came from his confidential agents intimations of attacks made on him at various points, which seemingly indicated an intimate knowledge of his most carefully guarded plans. This failure of secrecy was in itself sufficient to endanger the success of his great enterprise; with the inability to command ready money added, ruin seemed imminent.

Truscott had a large amount of securities, which in ordinary times would have been taken as collateral. But banks would not lend on them now at any rate of interest; in fact most of them could not, for they found it difficult to meet their own obligations, and more than one could not weather the storm. Truscott could not even sell his securities, except at a ruinous sacrifice, and at such prices as would produce only a fraction of what he needed. When every effort had been made, when no stone had been left unturned, Wendell Truscott was forced to face the alternative of ruin. In such a crisis, banks were as broken reeds, friendship was but a name, credit was paralyzed, and business at a standstill. Unless by a miracle he could raise two hundred thousand dollars in the next two days, his great enterprise would be a disastrous failure and bankruptcy would stare his company in the face. In this crisis of his career, Truscott's regret was less personal than artistic, as one might say. He knew his own powers, and had nothing to reproach himself with; but that a scheme of such magnitude and daring, worked up with to the very point of success, should fail from mere want of money, seemed almost ridiculous. It was as though an artist's dream of beauty should perish for lack of oil to mix his paints.

Truscott was so fully preoccupied during the day that he scarcely noticed his stenographer's absence from the office. He had received some letters in the morning mail, and had opened and read them hurriedly. The less important were laid aside. Those having any bearing upon the present crisis in his affairs were too important to await the slow course of the mails; they were answered by telegraph, by long distance telephone, or in person. Truscott was in the office scarcely more than half an hour between ten o'clock and three.

In the afternoon a meeting of the directors of the company was held in Truscott's office at which it was decided to wait until the last minute, and then, if no help were in sight, to make an assignment for the benefit of creditors.

XXVIII.

Stella, returning from the office with the papers, reached her boarding-house while tea was in progress. She did not feel like eating, but, lest her absence might attract attention, sat down among the other boarders and drank a cup of tea. She excused herself from an invitation to attend evening service at a neighboring church, and went to her room as soon as she left the supper-table.

She lit her reading lamp, and opening the packet of papers, took up the outer one, and read it through to the end. There were references she did not understand. Taking up the next, she found it of a date somewhat later, and referring to intermediate dates and occurrences.

"I had better," she thought, "arrange them first in chronological order."

She sorted out the mass of papers—they seemed quite numerous when laid loosely upon the table—in the order of their dates. They consisted of letters, memoranda, stock certificates and cancelled checks. Most of them were in her father's handwriting. Some were in Wendell Truscott's,—not the now bold and careless scrawl of the successful financier, but the more careful script of the clerk whose writing must pass under the eye of a superior.

Stella had sat down to her task with glowing anticipations. Visions of wealth and independence danced before her eyes. Her mother's hopes and her own would now be realized. Her interest in Truscott, her scruples, had been lost sight of in the glare of her successful discovery. She had the papers—the rest was mere matter of detail.

She read the first paper carefully. It was in her father's handwriting and was a memorandum or prospectus of a proposed commercial venture on a large scale; something indeed, on the order of the enterprise in which Truscott was at this moment engaged, but even wider in scope, and promising vaster returns than Truscott had figured.

"He has stolen my father's idea," she reflected, as she laid the paper down. "That proves nothing, but lays a good foundation. He is using the stolen idea now; the stolen money he has used from the beginning."

She took up the next paper. It was a memorandum of proposed articles of incorporation for a company to develop the scheme outlined in the first paper. By the prospectus, the preliminary organization was to be made by contract, secrecy being for a time one of the essentials to success; the incorporation was to follow as soon as the enterprise was fairly launched. In this second memorandum the contract was outlined upon the basis of a stock company. The amount named as the capitalization of the new company fairly took Stella's breath away. Ten million dollars! It was a large sum now; at the date of this paper it was stupendous! How much of this was her father's? He surely would not have undertaken to promote a scheme of this magnitude without a large personal interest.

The next document satisfied her curiosity upon this point. It was composed of several papers fastened together, and was evidently a draft of the proceedings in the organization of the corporation. Among the items was a list of subscriptions to capital stock, in which her father was set down as subscribing for twenty thousand shares at one hundred dollars each, making a total of two million dollars.

"And he died bankrupt," murmured Stella, with a rush of anger. "His confidential clerk, Wendell Truscott, has subscribed to twenty shares, and is rich."

Other paragraphs recorded the election of directors and officers. Her father was named as president of the new company. The other names were unfamiliar to Stella, and most of them were given as residents of New York.

The next paper was in the form of a letter, dated at New York, and addressed to Wendell Truscott, at Groveland. From it Stella gathered that her father had gone to New York to consult with certain capitalists. One of the paragraphs ran—

"I saw Burrows yesterday. He is positively dazzled with the enormous possibilities of the scheme! His idea is to enlarge the scope of the company, so as to take in not only the sources of supply of coal and oil and iron, but to secure the means of transportation. To do this will require enormous capital. I am to meet Millard and Joyce tomorrow. Burrows is going to see them, and arrange an interview, and I am to lay before them the details of the scheme."

Stella read the paper through with swelling heart. This was a father of whom one could well be proud! Wendell Truscott's great enterprise seemed but a mere tallow dip by the side of this brilliant conception of her father's genius. Stella now knew how she came by her intuitive grasp of figures and financial details, and her sense of fitness for high station. She was born to the purple!

Several letters followed separated in date by brief intervals, evidently forming one side of an active correspondence. Much space was devoted to details of the Groveland business, which, it appeared, had been left in Truscott's charge during her father's absence. It was quite evident that Mr. Merwin reposed great confidence in his managing clerk, and consulted him with reference to everything.

"I think you are too timid, Wendell," ran one paragraph of the next letter. "Normal youth is inclined to rashness, but your caution is rather suggestive of premature old age. One who would be a Napoleon of finance must be able to see a long way ahead, to form great combinations, to harmonize conflicting interests, to shape events and to forecast results! In this matter, Wendell, you are extremely shortsighted!

"We have decided to place the stock upon the market at par, as soon as we shall have secured the necessary options and contracts to insure success. The preliminary work will require great deal of money, which, of course the promoters must supply. I shall have to stretch my credit somewhat, but so certain are the results, and so enormous will be the profits—that I am sorry I have no more to invest. I have been spending the best part of my life working for a few paltry thousands a year, when millions were just as easily within my reach!"

The next letter was of similar tenor, relating in part to the further development of the new enterprise. Its tone intimated that Truscott had discouraged the extension of the new company into wider fields, and had raised some question about the men mentioned as willing to join it.

"You are wrong, Wendell, in your estimate of Royce. His connection with the *Credit Mobilier* was fully explained, and he was exonerated from any blame whatever. As to Millard it is true that the Western Pacific failed while in his hands, but by his consummate generalship the inevitable crash was deferred for several years, and its consequences rendered less disastrous. I have learned the inside history of these matters and know just where they failed. The facts, instead of discrediting these men, reflect great credit upon them."

There seemed at this point to be a gap in the correspondence as though a letter or letters were missing. Of the next communication, dated a week later, one paragraph ran as follows:—

"I am sorry, Wendell, that you wish to withdraw your subscription; but of course with your views I could not expect you to risk your money in the concern. I meant to do you a service, for of course your investment is not of great importance to the company in the way of capital. I think you will regret your action. But you will at any rate be on the safe side;—you will be sure of your four per cent in the savings bank. With us you might make four hundred per cent.

"Your action in this regard will not at all affect our present relations. I shall wish you to take even more complete charge of the Groveland business; and shall hope to find a larger opening for you in the new company, but of course, your position will be vastly different than if you were in on the ground floor."

Then came a bundle of stock certificates, representing a large amount of capital in the company. New and crisp, in all the bravery of bond paper and bank-note engraving, and green-and-gold ink, they seemed to radiate an atmosphere of affluence and enormous dividends. The very name of the concern, "The Universal Subterranean Development Company," was a spell to conjure with—an open sesame to unlock all the treasures of the earth, and pour them out into the lap of the beautiful and chastely draped goddess who posed in the center of the handsomely engraved certificate. Stella thrilled with exultation, as the figures marched before her eyes in stately array. These then were the documents that represented her father's wealth, and it was from these that Wendell Truscott had derived the capital with which he had built up his own enormous business!

The correspondence was resumed, after some lapse of time, her father in the meantime having returned home, and then gone a second time to New York. The tone of the correspondence had changed so radically as to confuse Stella, and she read several letters before the situation dawned upon her.

She gathered with gradually paling cheek and sinking heart, that her father had drawn largely upon the working capital of the Groveland business for investment in the new enterprise while yet in the chrysalis stage; that unforeseen difficulties had arisen; that her father, contrary to Truscott's urgent advice, had strained his credit to bolster up the newly formed company. Her father's associates had proved dishonest, and had dragged the unhappy man, almost desperate at the prospect of impending ruin, into courses passing the limit of strict honesty, and entering the shady borderland of the domain of crime.

She read her father's weak excuses, and noted how he leaned on Truscott for advice,—advice which he did not follow,—and had recourse to him for succor when involved in difficulties. The financial storm that broke over the country shortly before her father's death had swept away the poor remains of the Universal Subterranean Development Company, and with it the remnant of her father's once substantial fortune. Her father had collapsed under the weight of his misfortunes; and Truscott, aided by the general confusion attendant upon a great panic, beside which all lesser evils paled into insignificance, had succeeded in saving her father's good name from the greater obloquy that otherwise would have overwhelmed it.

There was more than one hiatus in the record Stella had perused. But these she was able to fill, partly from the knowledge of business methods acquired in Truscott's service, partly from things her mother had told her, and imagination easily supplied the rest.

For a while it required all of Stella's strength of mind to bear up under the crushing force of this discovery. Her first sensation was that of shame and grief at her father's weakness. Her god of gold had turned out to have hands of brass and feet of clay. Still to her memory a kind and loving father, a tender and devoted husband, he was no longer a hero and a saint, no longer that innocent victim of another's perfidy. Henceforth, pity, sorrow and regret, must share the love with which she would regard her father's memory.

Her next feeling was one of shrinking. The pride that had sustained the family in adversity was baseless. The bright flame of hope that had gilded the future was extinguished. Gone were all her dreams of wealth, of travel, of social freedom, of large and liberal culture! Now she could never play the lady bountiful, or hope to wander, save in imagination, through storied lands across the sea! She was only a working girl, and henceforth could look forward to no other career!

Gathering up the papers mechanically, she bound them together with the piece of red tape that had secured them. Through the small hours of the night, she lay awake, sick and sore of heart, until the tears came in an unrestrained flood. But when she had sobbed herself into something like composure, there came a sudden, sweet sensation of relief that it was all over, and of gladness that her search had not ended as she had thought it would; and ere she fell asleep Stella confessed to herself, for the first time, the reason why she thus welcomed the defeat of her most cherished hopes.

XXIX.

Stella awoke with a feeling of profound humiliation. For weeks she had been misjudging, and for part of that time holding in scorn and hatred her father's best friend. With returning day and a mind refreshed by sleep, her thoughts recurred to certain things which had not been entirely cleared up by her investigation of the night before.

Her mother had been receiving for many years a certain income, from a supposed remnant of her father's estate. It was possible that Wendell Truscott had been able to save this remnant for her mother, out of her father's property; but she remembered certain check-stubs in Truscott's safe, of which she had taken a memorandum. On footing the amounts of these for the period covered, she found them to aggregate substantially the total of her mother's income for the same time.

It needed but a confirmation of what this discovery suggested, to make her humiliation complete. She determined to know the worst at once.

"I shall ask Mr. Fitch about the facts," she thought. "We cannot conceal them any longer. We can never receive another cent of that money unless we are sure that it is our own."

As nearly as she could hope to see him, she was at the office of her father's executor. Fortunately he was in and disengaged.

"Good morning, Mr. Fitch," she said, as she entered the office.

He looked up, at first rather blankly, and then with a smile of recognition.

Ordinarily Mr. Fitch's smile would have been expansive and cordial; to-day it was a mere automatic contraction of the facial muscles, due to force of habit. For Mr. Fitch himself had been caught out in the financial storm, and was straining every nerve to make safe harbor. A lawyer by profession, he yet had large outside interests, and had accumulated a handsome fortune by judicious speculation.

"Oh, it's Miss Merwin!" he exclaimed. "You've grown so much since I saw you last that I hardly recognized you. It seems only a few years since you were a little girl in short skirts and long curls, and now you're a full-grown and properly dignified young lady—a very handsome one too, bless my soul!"

The compliment was also due to force of habit, for the old gentleman finished it with a sigh. It was sincere enough, in this instance, though he might have made it had she been less attractive. Now Mr. Fitch had made it a rule of his life always to "jolly" the women, and had rarely found his method fail to please.

"And how is your mother, Miss—Bella, is it? Ah, yes, Stella. How is your good mother?"

"She is quite well, sir. She would doubtless have sent her regards to you, if she had known I was coming. I have made this visit on my own account, Mr. Fitch."

"My dear young lady, what can I do for you? This confounded panic has pretty nearly done for me. But let us know what the trouble is, and if I can serve you I shall be glad to do so."

"I have recently come into the possession," replied Stella, "of information that leads me to suspect that my father left no property, and that the money paid to us through you since his death has not come from his estate. I beg you to tell me, sir, whether my notion is correct or not?"

Mr. Fitch glanced at her keenly, but manifested no great surprise.

"Well, well, Miss Merwin!" he said, "to whom could you owe your income but your father? Believe me, every cent of it has been the returns from an investment made by your father many years ago."

Stella felt relieved, but only for a moment. Mr. Fitch's manner was not convincing, and his statement left room for construction.

"There are investments *and* investments, Mr. Fitch. Tell me frankly—it is a matter of vital importance—whether or not Mr. Truscott has been paying us this money all these years?"

The old gentleman looked somewhat embarrassed under Stella's scrutiny, and did not answer for a moment.

"I don't remember," he said, finally, "whether I am under a promise of secrecy or not. But I certainly never meant to reveal the source of your mother's income, unless she should have pressed me for a final settlement of the estate—which she might have done, you know, at any time."

Stella listened with parted lips and straining heart. Her suspicions were confirmed.

"Then it *is* he on whose bounty we have lived all these years?" she demanded. She wished to realize the full depth of her humiliation.

"You seem determined, young lady, to have a categorical answer. An old fox of a lawyer like myself never likes to give a direct answer to a leading question. Witnesses are often the same way, though in their case it is more a matter of mental habit. I don't know anything more amusing, or more exasperating, as the case may be than to get one of these oblique thinkers on the stand, who answers every question with another, or—"

"Now, Mr. Fitch," interrupted Stella, reproachfully, "you're playing with me—and I won't be played with. You've deceived us all these years—of course with the best of intentions—and we have been living on charity, and misjudging the man whose bread we ate. We shall be too much ashamed ever to hold our heads up again."

"Bless my soul, young woman, you take things too tragically! and you are jumping to conclusions. I have n't said that Truscott gave you the money. But even assuming that he did, why feel so badly about it? Your father had given him his chance in life, and he may very properly have felt that to stand by his widow and orphans was merely repaying the debt. It would be a very fine thing for him to do,—mind you, this is only an assumption—and there are very plausible reasons even a high-spirited person like your mother, or yourself, might accept such a provision, for a time at least, as a loan, if not as a donation."

"The time is past, Mr. Fitch! We can never touch another cent of his money. I speak for mother as well as myself. The arguments that might have applied are no longer of any force. I shall write to Mr. Truscott and tell him we cannot accept it."

"Well, well!" said the old gentleman, rising as Stella rose to go, "I'm afraid you'll get me into trouble with Wendell. But wilful woman will have her way, and I never promised to lie about it, only not to volunteer information. A little harmless fencing with facts is quite in the way of a lawyer's business, who has to deal with all the different sorts of people who make up a world—but plain, unadorned lying is quite a different matter. I don't mind saying, Miss—er—ah—Della, that the money I have remitted to your mother came to me *through* Truscott."

"I knew it," murmured Stella. "It needed only this to"—

"But understand me," continued Mr. Fitch, impressively; "I don't know how the money came to him. There may have been some secret trust between your father and him—I can't say how that was."

"Good-bye, Mr. Fitch," said Stella, rising to go. "I think I understand it, perhaps better than you. We know you have acted with the best of intentions, but—mama will write to you. I cannot talk any more about the matter now."

"Well, goodbye, Miss—Ella. I'm afraid your browbeating of the witness has brought out some damaging admissions. But I'm in trouble anyway, and a little more won't affect the situation very seriously. Come and see me again,—if I live through this panic!"

But Stella's cup of humiliation was not yet full. On leaving Mr. Fitch's office she returned to her boarding-house, where she found two letters awaiting her that had come in the morning delivery. One was addressed in a female hand that seemed familiar; but upon glancing at the superscription of the other letter, in which she recognized the dashing and yet clerkly handwriting of her brother George, she laid down the first unopened. Her brother's letter ran as follows:—

"Skull-and-Crossbones, Dak.

"My dear Stella:—

"I have news for you! I have learned the name of my mysterious friend. You would never guess it!

"A week ago I met a fellow here whose face seemed familiar to me. He passed as a drummer for a tobacco house. I met him in town one day, and we fell into conversation, and to make a long story short, he turned out to be one of the officers who arrested me on that eventful night. We became sworn friends, and he told me in confidence that he was looking for Ross, *your* Ross, *my* 'Brown,' who had skipped with twenty thousand dollars of the company's money. Never until that moment had I fully realized what I had escaped! And my new, or rather my old acquaintance told me, too—I was never more surprised in my life-that my preserver was, of all people in the world, the bugbear of our youth, the family enemy and your present employer, Wendell Truscott!

"There is something sadly out of tune about our connection with this man, Stella. We have either been wrong in our notions about him—I never took much stock in them anyway—or else he has some darkly mysterious scheme of doing evil in the guise of good. I am willing to give him the benefit of the doubt, unless you have found out something to the contrary. He has rendered me a service of incalculable value,

and I am not able to figure out any profit to him in the transaction. I haven't written yet to thank him, as I don't wish to
give my informant away. I shall write sometime and acknowledge the obligation. And if you find that your trail ends in a
squirrel-track and runs up a tree, you can thank him for the
whole family,—if you think I'm worth the trouble.

"Love to mother. I'm doing well out here, and behaving
myself properly. You and mother need not be alarmed about
me. I have learned a lesson I shall never forget. A burnt child
dreads the fire.

"Lovingly
"George."

Stella could not imagine, after reading this letter, any lower
depth of self-abasement to which she could sink. The veil was
lifted still higher from her eyes, and her conduct for the past
few months appeared in what now seemed its true light—a
tissue of falsehood, treachery, and sheer dishonesty.

While in this frame of mind, it was almost mechanically
that she tore off the end of the other letter and began to read:

"My dear Miss Smith:—

"I send you by this mail, under another cover, two of your
shorthand note-books, which, knowing your orderly habits, I
presume you would like to place on file in their proper place.
One of them I carried away with me, *accidentally*, of course,
and the other came into my hands from another source.
Permit me to say that you write a very pretty shorthand; that it

is extremely legible and written strictly in accordance with the rules of your system,—which, by the way I used to teach,—and that your note-books proved exceedingly profitable reading; in fact I was paid five hundred dollars for transcribing their contents into ordinary English.

"I send these back purely as an act of friendship, for I like you very much indeed. They may possibly be called for at some time, and it might cause trouble for you, if you could not produce them. I am not afraid of your telling on me; for I don't live in Groveland, and my real name isn't Pearce, and you'll probably never see me again, and in this transaction you're as deep in the mud as I am in the mire. Be a good girl, take care of yourself, and don't be *too* confiding with strangers, or you are more than likely to be taken in. With renewed assurances of friendship, I remain,

"Yours reminiscently,
"Miss 'Pearce'."

When Stella had finished this letter she sat down and cried. Her other mistakes had been led up to by things for which she could hardly be held responsible. They had been errors of judgment, but they had not reflected any discredit on her own intelligence;—if her premises had been correct, her attitude toward Truscott would have been entirely logical. But this matter of Miss Pearce was entirely her own affair. She had prided herself on her intuition, and yet she had permitted herself to be fooled by the first person—one of her own sex, too—who had undertaken the task. Up to this time she had been able to cherish one comforting reflection,—that, after all she had done Mr. Truscott no harm, and that her efforts to learn the truth had set right a grievous misconception. Now even this solace was denied her. She had, unwittingly, it is true, but none the less certainly, betrayed her kind employer's confidence played into the hands of his enemies, and, for aught she knew, done him an irreparable injury.

XXX.

On the morning of the second day of the panic Truscott came down to his office a half hour earlier than usual. He had spent the evening at his club, hoping that he might see some way out of his difficulties. He clutched at several straws—but they were only straws. Of several men of large means whom he approached, men reputed to be possessed of much ready money, one confessed that he himself was hard pressed; the others made various excuses. Truscott perceived clearly that, for a day or two at least, there was no confidence between man and man. Those who could tide over the shoal might escape shipwreck,—those who could not must take the consequences. Truscott's affairs could not wait.

"If I cannot raise two hundred thousand dollars by three o'clock tomorrow," he had said to himself as he strolled slowly homeward up the avenue, after leaving the club, "I shall be ruined past recovery."

As became a strong man, he went to bed, slept soundly, rose early, and breakfasted, not quite with his usual appetite.

Arrived at the office, he took out his check-book and filled out a number of checks, mostly for small household and personal bills, among others one in favor of Mr. Fitch, for an amount equal to Mrs. Merwin's annual income. This he enclosed in an envelope with a note:

"Dear Mr. Fitch: I hardly need tell you to present this at once. Bank accounts are shaky affairs just now. This in confidence."

He called a district messenger. As the boy left the office with the note, the postman brought in the morning mail.

Truscott went through his letters rapidly, in the faint hope that they might contain something reassuring. They were mostly duns, or letters from agents, urging the necessity of prompt remittances, or giving notices of the approaching expiration of valuable options. Sick at heart he threw them aside one by one.

The last was in a larger envelope than the others, and was quite bulky. He turned it over mechanically. It was addressed in the handwriting of his absent stenographer, whom, in his extremity, he had almost forgotten. Wondering what she might have to write to fill so large an envelope, he tore open the package. It contained two letters, a couple of shorthand note-books, and a parcel of papers tied with a red ribbon. The letter he opened first and read as follows:—

"Dear Mr. Truscott:—In writing you this letter I am performing, by an effort of the will, the most difficult task I have ever undertaken. I thought, while in your office, that you had come to like me and to trust me; but it would be unfair for you to begin this letter with such an impression of my character. If I state the truth, and let you despise me from the beginning, you may then be less angry, for you will then know what to expect.

"Let me say, first, that I entered your office under a false name. I went there first by accident. I remained there deliberately, as a spy, intending to pry into your affairs and do you an injury. My zeal in your business was prompted more by the wish to understand it for my own purposes, than by the desire to serve you efficiently.

"I gained your confidence, and then abused it. I robbed your safe, and took from it the papers I return herewith.

"It is no palliation of my offence to say that my name is Stella Merwin, and that I acted on a misunderstanding; that I had been brought up to believe that you had ruined my father, and robbed his widow and children. A reluctant confession which I wrung from Mr. Fitch, my father's alleged executor,— the almoner of your bounty,—has confirmed my suspicions upon reading these papers: You have fed us and clothed us all these years! To your charity—no I will not use a term so much abused!—to your noble benevolence we owe the food we have eaten, the clothes we have worn, my brother's education and my own. Since reading these papers, I have also learned that to you it is due that my brother was saved from ruin and disgrace. During all these years, while you were loading us with benefits, we have misjudged you, reviled you, and hated you. I have spied upon and robbed my father's best friend. The letter

I enclose will show that even when I tried to be faithful, I did not succeed; I gave away your secrets, unknowingly, but perhaps quite as disastrously as though I had done so on purpose. I send you Miss Pearce's letter, that you may understand, in case any of your secrets have become known, to your injury, that *I* alone am to blame for it. You trusted me, and I was unworthy of your confidence.

"You may imagine my feeling when I learned from these papers that we owe you not only all these things but the salvation of my father's good name. You could not entirely conceal the truth, but you kept the facts from becoming public. I write this letter—not to thank you, for you could only scorn the empty phrases of a spy and a thief—but as a confession. The money you have given us I shall try to repay; from the debt of gratitude we owe you we could never be absolved.

"I shall not return to the office, for I would not dare to look you in the face again. I am going away from Groveland, for it is the scene of my crimes and humiliation. Future years may perhaps soften your anger and mitigate your scorn, and then you will think less unkindly of the wicked girl, who, though she deceived you and robbed you, yet did it ignorantly; and who sees in you the noblest and best of men, who, loving his friend once, loved him and his for all time, and for friendship's sake held up the hand that smote him, and warmed in his bosom the serpent that stung him to the heart. If you cannot forgive, then I shall hope that you will in time forget.

"Your unworthy but penitent 'typewriter,'
"Stella Merwin."

For a moment Truscott forgot his troubles and remembered nothing but the face of the absent girl. He was not angry. He had read Schopenhauer and Nordau, and had philosophical notions about the other sex, in the abstract. He even felt sorry for the poor girl, and sympathized with the soreness of her disappointment. The letter from Miss Pearce explained how certain of his plans had leaked out. The combined attack upon him all along the line, had doubtless been prompted by the knowledge gained from the letters contained in these note-books. The financial crisis had been simply an occasion—a better one could not have been imagined,—for bold and unscrupulous rivals to apply to his disadvantage the knowledge thus surreptitiously acquired. But the girl was not so much to blame; like himself she had simply been the victim of superior craft. It would be a lesson to them both, though Truscott smiled a sickly smile at the price of it.

To learn that she was the daughter of his former friend gave him a distinct thrill of pleasure, and explained too, a certain likeness that he had observed but had never been able to identify. He had loved his friend and benefactor; whether he had overestimated his obligations to Mr. Merwin, he had never stopped to figure out. For Wendell Truscott was one of those loyal natures, which, not lightly moved, never vary in their constancy. To have been his friend once was to be always his friend. To be loved by such a man meant a fidelity which neither absence, nor death, nor anything else, could alter or destroy. Wendell Truscott had not idealized Henry Merwin; but neither the reckless speculation, nor the disastrous failure, nor the pitiable weakness of Henry Merwin had been able to weaken Truscott's friendship. Even Merwin's weaknesses had strengthened Truscott's devotion, for they gave him the opportunity of self sacrifice. To so keen, so clear-sighted a business man, had come no thought of balancing benefits. To save his friend from ruin, to succor his family from grinding poverty, to rescue his son from disgrace, were simple elementary duties of friendship. That he should have been misjudged was a mere trifle, compared with the protection of the pride and self-respect of his friend's wife and children. He had even been thinking, in the event his great scheme proved successful, of increasing their allowance, if it could be done without awakening suspicion on their part as to its source.

He folded Stella's letter, and was in the act of placing it in his breast-pocket, when Johnnie entered the private office.

"Miss Wedderburn wants to know if she can see you, sir."

"Show her right in."

She came sailing into the room, like a noble ship across a swelling sea, freighted with love that spoke from her eyes and trembled upon her lips.

"Wendell," she cried, giving him both her hands with a warm, firm grasp, "I hear you are in trouble and need money. Take mine! I have two hundred thousand dollars in government bonds—I can lay my hand on them in five minutes. They are as good as gold! Take them and use them, and it will make me happy to have helped you!"

For a moment Truscott felt a wild leap of joy. A miracle had happened; relief was at hand; ruin was averted; his credit was saved; his great enterprise was assured!

She read his heart in his countenance, and she thrilled with love, and hope, and the happiness of serving him. But suddenly his face clouded; the light died out of his eyes. She looked at him wonderingly, with a vague sensation of alarm.

"Matilda," he said slowly, dropping her hands. "I"—

He could not say what was on his lips. He must temporize.

"I thank you from my heart, from my soul! But it is not certain yet that I shall need to avail myself of your kind offer. I have until three o'clock, and something may happen, something *must* happen before then, to relieve my embarrassment."

"You had better take it now, Wendell!"

"No, Matilda, I will not take it now. But later in the day, I will"—

"You will let me know?" she cried, "in time to help you? Promise me, Wendell, that you will let me hear from you before banking hours are over?"

"I shall be at home until two o'clock," she said, "and shall expect to hear from you before that time. Until then, good-bye—Wendell!"

She gave him her hand again, and let it linger in his clasp, and then she went out. As her carriage drove away, she threw a long backward look toward the upper window, near which sat the man she loved, and to whom she would freely have given herself and all that she possessed.

An hour passed. Another mail came in. There was nothing in it to improve the aspect of affairs, and more than one communication that made the outlook seem darker.

Truscott had been smoking furiously since Miss Wedderburn's departure. He threw his cigar away, and went out to lunch at a nearby restaurant, after which he went back to the office and smoked for another hour.

At two o'clock he drew a sheet of paper toward him and wrote the promised note:—

"Dear Miss Wedderburn:—I cannot accept your proferred aid. Believe me when I say that I fully appreciate your goodness, and that the offer is worth more to me to-day than it could ever possibly be under any conceivable circumstances. But while I thank you, I cannot accept it. I cannot tell you why; but it is better so.

"Yours with deepest gratitude,
"Wendell Truscott."

He rang the bell, and handed the note to Johnnie, with instructions to deliver it to Miss Wedderburn in person, without fail. He did not know that Matilda, in going out, had whispered to Johnnie, one of whose feet was already winged with memory, and the other with anticipation.

It was fifteen minutes walk to Miss Wedderburn's; Johnnie made it in ten.

Miss Wedderburn read the note hastily, seized a pen and dashed off the following reply: it came hot from the heart, and she did not stop to read it over after it was written.

"Dear Wendell:—I know your reason, and I appreciate the nobility of your thought! You will not take the money because you cannot take the woman with it! I am only a woman, but I can be as noble as you! Take the money, and take the other woman! I have learned who she is, as I presume you have or will; I loved her mother once, and I give you up to the daughter.

"I enclose a check. Take it and use it, if you value our friendship! I can give up my love for you, Wendell—I am not ashamed to speak it, for you must have read my heart long, long ago—but I cannot lose my friend! I shall always sign myself, as I do now,

> "Sincerely your,
> "Matilda Wedderburn."

Her carriage was in waiting. She entered it with Johnnie.

"Drive fast," she said to the coachman, "as fast as the law will permit!"

The carriage whirled down the avenue. At the next corner a runaway horse, attached to a huckster's wagon, darted at right angles across the avenue, and ran a wagon shaft into the shoulder of one of Miss Wedderburn's grays. She sprang out, with Johnnie after her.

"Do what is best, Johnson," she said to the coachman. "I cannot stop."

She glanced at her watch. It was half past two.

They started at a rapid walk, and at the next corner caught a street-car on the track turning into the avenue there. They reached the El Dorado Building at a quarter of three.

Miss Wedderburn handed Johnnie the letter she had written, with which she had enclosed another paper. "Give it to Mr. Truscott, Johnnie, and then come back to me."

The elevator shot Johnnie to the eighth floor in one minute or less. Truscott was sitting at his desk, smoking furiously, and watching the clock, like a prisoner condemned to death awaiting the hour of execution. That fateful finger, moving slowly but surely, would soon mark the hour of his doom.

"In fifteen minutes," he said to himself, "I shall be a ruined man, with a promising past behind me, a doubtful future before me. I wonder if this cigar will be finished before I am?"

He threw a glance at the clerks in the outer office.

"Poor devils," he murmured, kindly, "they'll be out of a job tomorrow!"

He looked back at the clock, and at that moment Johnnie entered the office with a letter.

He opened it curiously, and read it at a glance. The paper enclosed was a certified check, payable to his order, for two hundred thousand dollars. Miss Wedderburn had changed her bonds into money, which was still to be had for absolutely unquestioned securities, and the check was in such shape that he could use it without a moment's delay, in spite of the large amount represented.

Truscott sprang to his feet.

"If I could love two women, this would be one of them!" he said to himself. "Such a letter admits of but one response. Such a friendship is too rare to be spurned!"

He seized his hat and ran for the elevator. It was five minutes walk from the El Dorado Building to the bank where his most pressing obligations were due.

At one minute to three the check was deposited and his notes provided for. He was saved!

XXXI.

The next day Truscott called at Miss Wedderburn's residence.

"Miss Wedderburn is slightly indisposed," said the maid who had announced him, "and begs that you will excuse her today."

He went away with a certain sense of relief. He had performed what might have proved a difficult duty; but the lady's tact had robbed the situation of its awkwardness. That he should have overlooked for so many years this jewel among women, to discover her surpassing excellence only when too late, was a freak of Fate beyond his comprehension. He could give her every return but love. From this time forth, the word "woman" had a new meaning for Wendell Truscott;—for him Matilda Wedderburn had glorified her sex forever.

He wrote her a frank and manly letter, in which he mentioned their long friendship, which had culminated in the great service she had rendered him. He had accepted her aid in the spirit in which it was offered. He hoped to repay the loan within a few days. The obligation he would regard as no burden, but as a priceless memory. As soon as she would permit him, he hoped to say by word of mouth what he could only faintly and coldly express in written words.

He received, several days later, a reply, dated at New York. Miss Wedderburn, in a few gracious phrases, acknowledged the receipt of his letter and expressed her satisfaction at having been able to serve a friend of so long standing. She was going abroad, she said, to spend the Winter in Spain and along the Mediterranean—possibly might go as far as Egypt—and she hoped to see Mr. Truscott on her return the following Spring. The money she had loaned him could be repaid to her business agent at Mr. Truscott's convenience, or he could even retain it, if he saw fit, until her return. She wished him a happy issue out of all his difficulties, and success in all his enterprises, which she understood were of a magnitude befitting a commanding intellect, such as she had long recognized in him.

Taken as a whole, it was a charming letter. Not one word of it suggested unrequited love, or disappointed hopes, or tragic renunciation. It was a triumph of perfect breeding, a marvel of epistolary taste. It made Truscott feel small and mean and unworthy. He would not be a fitting husband for such a woman. The best and wisest man on earth would be none too good for her.

Stella had left her Groveland boarding-house and returned to Cloverdale. She had not quite decided upon her future course.

That she must work for her living was certain. She did not wish to follow, in Groveland, the business that had led her into such a thorny path—she would have lived in constant dread of meeting the man she had misjudged and injured. She had hoped—she had hardly dared to hope—that he might write a line,—he had been so magnanimous!—that he might vouchsafe some word to lighten in however small a measure the burden of shame and remorse that oppressed her. He might forgive her the injury, the injustice,—but of course it was too much to hope that he could ever overlook the concealment, the gross treachery that had marked her conduct; however broad his charity, he could never do less than despise her. It might be a pleasure to look at him now and then, if she herself could remain unseen; but to run the risk of meeting him face to face, of being scorched by the scorn and contempt of his stern eyes, was more than she could ever endure. She knew where a teacher was needed for a small country school. Her business career in the city had proved a lamentable failure. She would try again, in a humbler sphere, more suited to her character and capacity.

She was preparing to act upon this conclusion when she received one day a letter. Her heart beat tumultuously at the sight of her name on the cover—her real name, "Miss Stella Merwin," in Truscott's handwriting. It was happiness to know that he had answered her letter, no matter what the contents. If he should reproach her,—if he should heap upon her all the harsh names her conduct merited,—it would yet be a pleasure to read them; they would seem some expiation of her crime. She opened the letter and devoured it with eager eyes, that, ere she finished it, were filled to over-flowing.

"Dear Miss 'Smith':—

"Since you left me so abruptly I have fallen away behind in my correspondence. I have tried several stenographers, but none of them suit me. I am afraid you have spoiled me by your excellent work. I really do not see how I can get along without you,—now or ever hereafter. Come back to me, dear child, or let me come to you, and we will part no more forever, so long as we both shall live.

"Faithfully yours,
"Wendell Truscott."

A Business Career is the story of Stella Merwin, a white woman entering the working-class world to discover the truth behind her upper-class father's financial failure. A "New Woman" of the 1890s, Stella joins a stenographer's office and uncovers a life-altering secret that allows her to regain her status and wealth.

When Chesnutt died in 1932, he left behind six manuscripts unpublished, *A Business Career* among them. Along with novels of Paul Laurence Dunbar, it is one of the first written by an African American to cross the color line and write exclusively about the white world. It is also one of only two Chesnutt novels with a female protagonist.

Rejecting the novel for publication, Houghton Mifflin editor Walter Hines Page encouraged Chesnutt to try to get the book in print. "You will doubtless be able to find a publisher, and my advice to you is decidedly to keep trying till you do find one," he wrote. Page clearly saw that in *A Business Career* Chesnutt had written a successful popular novel grounded in realism but one that exploits elements of romance.

Charles W. Chesnutt (1858–1932) was an innovative and influential African American writer of the late nineteenth and early twentieth centuries. His novels include *The House Behind the Cedars*, *The Marrow of Tradition*, *The Colonel's Dream*, as well as the posthumously published novel *Paul Marchand, F.M.C.* from University Press of Mississippi.

MATTHEW WILSON has written introductions to *A Business Career*, *Evelyn's Husband*, and *Paul Marchand, F.M.C.*, and is the author of *Whiteness in the Novels of Charles W. Chesnutt*, all from University Press of Mississippi. He is associate professor of humanities and writing at Penn State University, Harrisburg. MARJAN A. VAN SCHAIK edited both *A Business Career* and *Evelyn's Husband* along with Wilson and is a part-time instructor at Millersville University.

CPSIA information can be obtained
at www.ICGtesting.com
Printed in the USA
JSHW050812230222
23218JS00001B/64